TUCSON TALES

Bohemians,
Bolsheviks
and
Border Rats

TUCSON TALES

Bohemians, Bolsheviks and Border Rats

Harvey Burgess

SUNSTONE PRESS

SANTA FE

Sunstone books may be purchased for educational, business, or sales promotional use.
For information please write: Special Markets Department, Sunstone Press,
P.O. Box 2321, Santa Fe, New Mexico 87504-2321.

Book and Cover design › Vicki Ahl
Body typeface › Constantia
Printed on acid-free paper
∞

Library of Congress Cataloging-in-Publication Data

Burgess, Harvey, 1960-
  [Short stories. Selections]
  Tucson tales : bohemians, Bolsheviks and border rats / by Harvey Burgess.
    pages cm
  ISBN 978-0-86534-927-8 (softcover : alk. paper)
  1. Tucson (Ariz.)--Fiction. 2. Short stories, American. I. Title.
  PS3602.U7454T83 2013
  813'.6--dc23

                        2012050465

WWW.SUNSTONEPRESS.COM
SUNSTONE PRESS / POST OFFICE BOX 2321 / SANTA FE, NM 87504-2321 /USA
(505) 988-4418 / ORDERS ONLY (800) 243-5644 / FAX (505) 988-1025

Dedication

This book is dedicated to the memory of my father, John Burgess,
and to my wife, Ülkü.
Without both of them, I would never have come to the USA
and to Tucson, Arizona.

Thanks

Special thanks to the following: My friend and fellow writer, Jonathan Kaplan, who has been my mentor throughout this project and has invested many hours in it. My editors, Dr. Hillary Tiefer of Pen and Ink Editing and Kirsten Voris.

Thanks also to Joan Harris, Richard Franz, Tolga Cavcav, Natalie Brown, Dr. Barbara Eiswerth, Mario M. Sainz, Jack Nestor, Claudia Arevalo, Robert Anthony Villa, Jill Wristen, Jazmyn Chymere, Naima Hana, David Shoopman, John Carr and Scott Petersen; my brothers, Paul and Andy, and my mother, Lana, for their unstinting support.

Zev Rubin for the front cover photograph and Sheri Laizer for allowing me to use her poem in the "Love Letters From A Bandit" story.

Preface

I fell in love with Tucson the minute I arrived there in October 2006. I found its landscapes beguiling, its climate amazing and its people friendly and down to earth. After London, the slow pace of life was also most agreeable.

Most of all, it was the diversity of both the city and its occupants that captivated and inspired me. Every day I would be awe struck by something I'd seen-whether it be an animal, a plant or a piece of urban iconography- or someone I'd met. All of humankind rubs shoulders in this magical Old Pueblo. Whatever you're into, there's something here for you.

Being here immediately stimulated my creative juices and, for five and a half years, the words have flowed as never before.

Writing *Tucson Tales* and exploring every nook and cranny of Tucson in the process has been a wonderful experience and I feel very privileged to have had the opportunity to do it.

18,000 Costa Rican Dollars

August 2009

Ten to six a.m. The outsized spliff drooped from Larry Love's mouth. Three or four strands of tobacco had somehow worked their way through the roach and were now tangled up in his wispy, ginger-grey moustache. He hoped the stuff described as "powerhouse" by the vendor—his face conveying numerous exclamation marks—would soon relieve the murderous itch emanating from his red, raw groin.

He had not the faintest idea what had caused the ailment. Otherwise, the most likely culprit had been sex, but he hadn't had any for over three months. He wondered if the ninety-nine cent boxers he'd bought from the thrift shop opposite Walgreens at St. Mary's Plaza had been full of disease. He told himself, Sonofabitch! I'm gonna go back in there and ask those people if they wash the clothes they hawk thirdhand!

He was comforted somewhat, however, by the memory of the last time he had a rash, all around his neck, after being stung by a wasp. He had scored some unbelievable caked Ethiopian cannabis the day before and it had worked marvels. The pain had disappeared immediately and had never come back. True, he only had some grass from *pinche* Nogales this time. But he was still confident of the healing properties of The Weed, as long as it was...The Weed. This stuff was full of little un-Weed like twigs and seeds, but....

One thing was for sure. The cathartic environment of Tucson's Sweetwater Wetlands near the interstate that cut through the side of the city had never let him down. He would never forget the first time he sought refuge there, some thirty years ago. His drunken father had beaten him for alleged disrespect, two days after his eighth birthday, and he'd run out of the house and then hid in the wetlands for a week, where he'd survived on blackberries and rainwater. He probably would have stayed there longer had not a lone birdwatcher, who politely and cheerily informed him he was from someplace that sounded like "Lestuhshuh" over in England, discovered him crashed out in a ten foot high reed bed.

"HUL-lo. D'ya need some help now, lad?"

What this high-toned foreign speaker was doing in Tweekersville-Thousand-Yard-Stare-Redneck Tucson was mysterious. Larry distinctly remembered the timid, nasal voice flung at him as he tried hard to loosen his numbed jaw and open his conjunctivitis-ridden eyes. He raised his arm, and the man pulled him up and then provided some hot coffee and a cheese, ham, and pickle sandwich. Good man.

When Larry's mother picked him up from the hospital, the reek of alcohol on her breath had nearly knocked him down. He was fixated by the blue skull and crossbones on her chunky forearm as she dragged him along the road. He didn't say a word for a month.

The next time anyone pulled a slumbering Larry up out of difficulty of some kind was two years later. This time it was a firefighter, who rescued him from his second floor bedroom as the rest of the apartment burned down. His mom had left the gas on just before crashing out on the kitchen floor. If his equally inebriated father had had enough gray matter left after a lifetime of substance abuse, he might not have crawled out of bed, placed a fag between his lips, and tried to light a match three times at the kitchen door without either smelling the gas or seeing his wife prostrate on the linoleum. The fourth attempt to destroy the place was successful, and the whole building was blown sky high. Larry became an orphan at ten. He inherited a wheelbarrow full of sand and a bottle opener, which the neighbor had borrowed and then returned after hearing the bad news.

But that was then.

After the medication had done its work on the rash, Larry already felt lucky. He sensed, somehow, something was coming along—though what it was he had no idea.

Right on cue, though, in what he took to be a gesture of solidarity, one of Larry's favorite birds, the imperious red-winged blackbird, made a grand entrance. It glided across the turquoise pond, no more than a foot above the water, before rising steeply in an arc, grazing the top of the palm tree as it soared up, up, and away. Red black, red black, red black, red black. Tantalizing glimpses of impressionistic color, all too elusive. It was like someone was flicking a whole bunch of movie stills in front of his face. "You know, when I die I'd really dig coming back as a bird in the next life. Must be kinda liberating," he said to himself.

And then the Heath Robinson cooler in his home—a converted school bus—which had been out of action for a good month suddenly began chugging. The clock on the dashboard, which, for some reason, always kept working, read six a.m..

Initially, the contraption spewed out a load of dust and dead flies, but soon the cold air was running up Larry's naked, knife-scarred body, and he felt his dick stir as the draught hit it. Not that his regular-as-clockwork dawn woodie needed any prompts. As far as he knew, his friends had all stopped waking up hard in their teens. To paraphrase Larry's attitude on the issue: if the Lord wants to grant me more than my fair share of nookynook, I'm ready to accept his benevolence with good grace.

Every day at around noon, Larry headed down to the wasteland near the interstate's slip road, which ran, straight and useless to most ordinary citizens, alongside the railway tracks. For eleven years this had been part of his daily itinerary, proof positive that anyone could be a creature of habit. In fact, Larry reckoned the number and rigidity of his daily tasks would exceed those of your run- of-the-mill bank manager or insurance salesman. Sure, they almost certainly had their morning showers, lunch hours, and business meetings. But he bet they did not wake up at 5:30 a.m., scrounge in dumpsters, feed dogs, cats, hens, hamsters, and snakes at seven each morning, read science fiction novels between eight and ten, skin up at eleven, look for discarded items and general detritus between twelve and two, plumb in a toilet, dig a trench for a cable, install a starter motor between two and five, sculpt a Mayan head from a block of stone between five and nine, nor cook rabbit or duck on a skewer over a campfire between nine and midnight.

The revived vehicle permitted him to make his way to one of his favorite dumpsters. There he found two stainless steel dessert spoons, two copper tubes, a broken record player, and an unused can of silver grey paint. Then it happened. He clapped his eyes on a black sports bag with a single bright orange stripe running across it. Holy fucking shit. Inside it were four bundles of banknotes. Four rubber-banded decks of-holy-fucking-shit-money. Holy fucking shit.

(To say Larry felt a frisson of excitement run through him, as the cheery concerned Brit who had popped up those many years ago in Larry's life might have put it, does not capture the sensation. The most valuable thing Larry had ever found before was four-hundred and forty-eight dollars, which he had blown within two hours on dope and a greyhound; weird how you never think you're going to find, accidentally, *money*.)

What have we here? Jesus Christ... Lordy, Lordy, Lordy.... The words pummeled through his consciousness. Are you hallucinating again, Larry boy, or is this some serious, ah, windfall here? He felt he was bordering on delirious. He was already thinking about the secondhand Winnebago he'd had his eye on.

As he tore the elastic band off the first bundle, it never occurred to him that the money would not be U.S. dollars. At first glance, continuing to say holy shit to himself, he saw the "100" in the top left hand corner and the moustache on the face of a bald bureaucrat or politician.

But then, as it insinuated itself into his consciousness that the pol didn't look like any U.S. dollar father of the country he knew of, ah, shit, no, he saw and then spelled out what must have been some kind of Spanish or something, "B-A-N-C-O C-E-N-T-R-A-L D-E C-O-S-T-A R-I-C-A" along the bottom. Bank... of...*Costa Rica?!?!*

Fuck it. Costa Rican dollars?! Oh well.

Doubt they're worth diddly. But look at them. They're brand new. Mint condition. Nice color as well. Pink and green. Suppose I should take them to a bank and see what they say, he said to himself.

That night the heavens opened. The monsoon season had begun. For at least twelve years, Larry, Chester, and Sonny had celebrated its arrival in what they called The Spectacular Dome on the grounds of Tucson's Manning House, a magnificent mansion built in 1907 in the Spanish colonial style in which Levi

Manning, the then mayor of Tucson, had lived. It was situated in an upscale downtown district which used to be known as Snob Hollow on account of all the local dignitaries who built their houses there. The lush grounds, full of lemon, orange, and grapefruit trees, represented a veritable oasis in the desert, as far as Larry was concerned. And the dome was one of his all-time favorite hangouts. It formed the portico at the building's front entrance, was decorated with exotic plants, flowers, and various imperious, pheasant-like birds and dotted with semi-circular skylights.

To be there and flying high, at the height of a monsoon storm, was indescribably good. The amazingly loud thunderclaps, echoing inside the dome, the flashes of lightening shooting through the skylights, as though God was poking his incandescent fingers through them, and the dancing birds on the ceiling, were, for Larry, the very affirmation of being alive. "When I die, I wanna come back as one of those birds—they look like they're having a riot," Larry announced.

He then made his nightly toast. "Ladies and gentleman. Please be upstanding and raise your glasses to our esteemed forebears here in Snobby Hollow, most notably our much-esteemed former Mayor, Levi Manning, and his architect, Mr. Trost, without whom we would not be experiencing the sensual pleasures of our heavenly dome, a truly sacred spot for us three sons of Tucson."

The three of them raised their cans of Heineken, clunk them together, and downed the remaining contents as one. Then they passed around the joint.

"Are those venerable gentlemen cringing or chuckling as they look down on us now?" said Sonny, the intellectual.

"Good question, Sonny. Hopefully we'll find out when it's our turn to meet our maker," said Chester. "And allow me to raise another toast to Mr. Love and his Costa Rican booty. Here's hoping he gets some good news from the bank tomorrow."

"Thanks, Chester. But I'm not holding my breath. Who knows if security will even let me through the door? Think I'll put my leather headband on, though. Got to look the part."

The three of them burst into hysterical laughter and were too busy cackling away, ten minutes later, to notice the javelina which was staring at them intently from a distance of ten feet.

"Can I help you...sir?" The twinkling female greeter in the Bank of America downtown branch looked Larry over. Larry was aware that the brown leather, lattice headband, twelve-inch beard, and worn sandals made him look distinctly, possibly awesomely, Christ-like. He guessed she would have bet a hundred bucks that he was cashing in a big bag of pennies that he had accumulated over a period of years. They must have at least five down and outs in there every year with piles and piles of coppers. Larry had heard one of them walked out with a cool twelve hundred bucks. Did the greeter reckon that penny collecting should be classified as a job and subject to tax?

"Hello there, miss. Yes, I certainly hope so. Look, to cut to the chase, I found eighteen thousand Costa Rican dollars, eighteen thousand. I counted 'em down by the railway tracks and, well, I need to find out what you can give me for them."

"I see, sir. Can I just clarif...?"

"Look, I'm not saying they're gonna buy me that Winnebago on the lot at Grant and Kolb. You know, the one opposite Whataburger. But they might be able to fix me up with a re-conditioned cooler unit. I got my eye on one over at ....He felt her breathy smile and perfect demeanor shine on him. Trained puppy dog.

"That's fine, sir. Would you like to take a seat over there, and I'll have someone come talk with you."

"Fine with me!"

Actually, this was the first time Larry had ever set foot in a bank. He had collected eight hundred seventy-four dollars in pennies and had planned to cash them in when he reached a grand. Although he had always assumed when he got to the thousand he would just walk into the bank and back out with the cash, nothing to it, now it felt...really weird to be actually inside a bank. For one thing, there were no animals and, for another, it was freezing, like being in a cold storage unit. Jeez, how do these folks stand it?

"Sir?" the greeter cooed. "Mr. Cruz of our foreign currency section will be with you soon. Oh, and what did you say your name was again?"

"It's Larry. Larry Love."

"Oh, that's a nice name! Doubt anyone's ever forgotten it. Am I right?"

"Yeh, miss. You're dead right. Larry Love from Lubbock, I sure ain't easy to forget."

Larry got such a good vibe from the greeter that he almost hit her with his favorite chat-up line: "When you and me gonna get busy, baby?" It almost never worked, but he didn't much care. He loved delivering it and it always got a laugh. On one occasion, he'd tried it with a girl at the cash register at a K-Mart, whose peroxide hair was laced with wisps of pink and purple and who had a cleavage so deep Larry asked her if his hamster could hibernate in it for the winter. She'd laughed so uncontrollably, everything jiggling, that she was unable to serve the other people waiting in line for a good couple of minutes. When asked by her employer what she had found so funny, she replied, "Dunno, really. Everything. The way he just came out with it. And the way he looks. I mean, he couldn'ta had a bath in a month and a haircut in ten years."

Mr Cruz would look into the matter. He'd contact the Costa Ricans to establish whether they had any knowledge of the missing bank notes. Larry was asked to come back a week later.

"Hello there, Mr. Love, and how are we today? Mr. Love, I have some news for you. Do please take a seat."

"It's okay, Mr. Cruz, I'm good standing." Larry felt just as uncomfortable on his second visit to the bank as he had on the first one. If he'd known anyone he could trust they would've been there in his place.

"No problem, Mr. Love."

"Larry, just Larry," Larry said.

As if not hearing, the little mustachioed man was saying that those colons from 1992 were obsolete but....

"Ah, excuse me, sir. What are *colums*?

"*Colons*, Mr. Love. The Costa Rican currency is called the *colon*. Anyway, the notes you found had never actually been in circulation. They were stolen from a house belonging to an ex-governor of the Bank of Costa Rica, in the capital, San Jose, in 1994. He himself had stolen them and was in jail at the time on charges of embezzlement and corruption. However, the Central Bank offered a substantial reward for their return because they could have been used as evidence in the case against the governor.

"Reward?" Larry tugged at his beard and felt a hair remain in his clenched fist. "How much might they be offering for these co-loans?"

"Ah, well, Mr. Love, it seems the offer is no longer on the table."

"Oh, jeez. Might I ask why not, sir?"

The little man was smiling.

"Because they closed the case. The governor died during the trial. However, however! The Costa Ricans are still interested in recovering the notes. The fact that they are in mint condition and numerically sequential makes them somewhat unique. They would like to display them in the national museum."

"Ah. So let me get this straight, Mr. Cruz. They didn't want them back but now they do. For a museum." Larry could feel his head shaking. "Okay, so what will they give me for them?"

"Well, they've made two suggestions. If we simply send them back, they will pay five hundred dollars. Alternatively, if you prefer to deliver them in person to the Central Bank, they will cover your travel expenses and issue you a three month visa to visit Costa Rica, and, as they told me to tell you, you'll get to experience firsthand their wonderful, tourist-friendly country."

When Larry, Sonny, and Chester next met up for the Splendor Dome Event, Larry handed them a page torn from some newspaper. The other two observed that Larry looked both more suntanned and well-fed than usual. But on his face was an expression of permanent shock.

May 15, 2010
Costa Rican Herald

An American citizen by the name of Larry Love was deported yesterday after serving two weeks in prison. He had been convicted of criminal trespass and possession of five grams of marijuana after being discovered living clandestinely, with a dog and a hen, on the grounds of Calderon Mansion House, the residence of the Director of the National Museum. The strangest thing about the whole affair was the fact that he was known to the director as the person who had found, in Tucson, Arizona, the 18,000 unused colons which are now on display in the museum and returned them in person to the director.

A mere three months later, Sonny and Chester sat solemnly in the Splendor zone. They had just scattered Larry's ashes on the hallowed ground. One minute he's in the world, larger than life, entertaining them with his silvery tongue and the next, he's gone. Plucked from Planet Earth without so much as by your leave. Fifty-one years old. Brain Hemorrhage. Young by middle class standards but not by those of the underclass they belonged to. No one they knew ever lived beyond sixty. It was just too punishing an existence, and none of their kind ever had a salaried job, an apartment, or a credit card, let alone health insurance. But they were still shocked. Larry was the most active person they'd ever known, a huge personality. Without him, there was such a huge void. Life would never be the same again.

As they reflected on their loss, they heard a loud flapping of wings. Hovering above one of the skylights was a bird. A striking black hawk. Sonny and Chester looked at each other, the hair on their necks standing on end. They knew immediately who it was.

Arthur, The Late Starter

Arthur Robertson was one of life's late starters. At thirty-one he lost his virginity. At forty, he began writing poetry. At fifty-five, he became a palm reader. At sixty-three, he rode a motorbike for the first time. At seventy, he learnt to cook and at seventy-eight, he started playing the harmonica. Now, at eighty-three, he was learning Spanish and toying with the idea of taking up tennis. All of which prompted him to ask himself, fairly regularly, what he had done for the first thirty years of his life. The answer did not come readily.

Whenever Arthur cast his mind back to his first three decades it reminded him of watching one of those silent family films on Super 8. The grainy images in his mind certainly stimulated a degree of neuronal activity, yet there was some kind of malfunction in the wiring. The cognitive function appeared to be out of sync with the visual hardware. He remembered spending the first twelve years of his life in a trailer park on Grant Road, and he recalled that there was a decrepit saguaro with its innards exposed and a skull and crossbones carved into its base, just to the left of the entrance to the lot. But he could not for the life of him summon up the inside of the trailer or the vehicle in which the family travelled.

Every so often, random images of the Tucson of a bygone age would appear in Arthur's mind. He recalled meeting a pasty-faced, harmonica-playing, Scottish tuberculosis patient, one of many hundreds who flocked to the Old Pueblo for treatment. He remembered the Twinburgers and the root beer at Bokes Drive-In on North Stone, and seared into his memory was the time he ran into a desperate Hispanic family down by the railway station. They'd been evicted from their house in Barrio Viejo, part of a mass demolition due to the huge urban renewal that took place in the fifties and sixties. He helped smuggle them onto a goods train and gave them his rare Civil War era New York Officer's coat button, which he reckoned was worth at least twenty bucks.

Arthur's recollections of his siblings were sketchy, to say the least. He remembered a much older brother called Vince who used to visit periodically. Vinny, as he was known, always wore black dungarees and had webbed feet. Arthur thought that he may have worked on the railroads in Louisiana but he was far from certain. There were two younger siblings, although they had a different mother and he rarely saw them. One was a very fat, freaky girl whose principal preoccupation was collecting dead insects. She would carry them around in a matchbox and set them out on an old chess board as if they were toy soldiers in battle formation. The other was lanky and paper thin. All that Arthur could remember of him was that he could not say his r's properly. He used to ask for "extwa wations" at which the sister would giggle hysterically.

What Arthur did know was that his father built electrical circuits and repaired radios. He worked in a rickety lean-to behind the trailer which emitted a pungent odor of burning metal. Arthur could picture his bald, egg-shaped head as he hunched over the work surface, solder in hand, cigarette drooping from his thick, mauve lips. As for his mother, Arthur's abiding memories of her were her green floral apron, her comely bosom in which he would often nestle, her rat-a-tat laugh, and her chicken broth, with its generous allocation of Brussels sprouts.

When Arthur was thirteen he left his native Tucson and went to work for a distant relative in a Californian vineyard. It was the height of the prohibition era, and the demand for home-brewing went through the roof. For the ensuing twenty years, aside from being able to prune, thin, and cajole a grapevine along a trellis, the only thing that Arthur could usefully do was to hop freight trains to Tucson and back. At thirty, he had acquired no real sense of self and had no conception of an overriding objective in life. But his thirty-first and thirty-second years would shape his character for the rest of his life. To say that he underwent a metamorphosis would in no way be to engage in hyperbole.

The first thing that happened was that Arthur was seduced by the barber's wife, a buxom red-head who was twenty years his senior. It happened suddenly, on a blustery Monday afternoon, in the woods behind the train station. The attraction was instant and not a word was uttered. There were none of the usual furtive glances. Mrs. Powers simply beckoned to him to follow her. He had a vivid recollection of the mud spattering on the backs of her fishnet stockings, while her white stilettos squelched as they bored into the earth. The sex itself was short but very, very sweet. Arthur had allowed himself to be led every step of the way and, miraculously, for the first time ever, he shed his inhibitions.

Prior to Mrs. Powers, there had been several abortive attempts at copulation. Arthur would always be overwhelmed by nerves and would just turn to jelly. There are some men who need their sexual partner to take control and Arthur was one of them. The funny thing was that it was only when Arthur saw the question, "Do you like outdoor sex?" in a magazine some eight years later that he came to realize that it carried with it a certain cachet—not unlike being a member of the "mile-high club." Later in life, as an enlightened, largely self-taught man—he would become a prodigious reader— sex would be much less important to Arthur than it was to most men—he would view it as a pleasant occasional diversion but agreed with Aristotle that it represented a threat to rationality. But he always remained grateful to Mrs. Powers for the initiation, for it was she who opened up the world of intimacy for him, not to mention an appreciation of his own body.

Several weeks after his encounter with Mrs. Powers, Arthur met the man who was to launch him on a life-long journey of spiritual discovery. In keeping with most things in Arthur's life, the nature of his meeting with Guru Srikanth was somewhat unusual. While slumbering on the sodden wood floor of a goods train, he opened his eyes and saw an Asian man with long, straggly hair who was dressed in a white robe and flip-flops. The man was sitting cross-legged and rocking gently back and forth. His eyes were shut. Arthur studied the man for quite a while but nothing changed. He then nodded off again, and when he awoke, he looked over again and the man continued to perform the same movement in metronomic fashion. At one point, Arthur toyed with the idea of "waking" the man up but he thought better of it.

Ten hours later the pair of them were sharing a marijuana cigarette in a Tucson squat, amidst a motley group of bohemians, hobos, and drifters. On that very first day, Srikanth began teaching Arthur how to meditate, how to breathe, how to allow his thoughts to run free, how to move gracefully and with great economy, how to live frugally and minimalistically, and how to appreciate the infinity of the cosmos and the divine. It was all so marvelous and revelatory; Arthur felt like a totally different person.

Srikanth had apparently arrived in the Land of the Free a week after Hitler took power in Germany, on a boat from Delhi and in possession of a six-month visa, but had never left. The closest he had ever come to being picked up by the cops was when he was reprimanded for entering a church in New Jersey bare-chested, in the fall of 1983.

Srikanth was a self-styled guru who described himself as "one who is availed of unconditional, undifferentiated, self-validated, direct perception." He was a devotee of Mahavira, the Indian sage who lived in the sixth century BC and whose philosophy underpins the religion of Jainism.

As for Arthur, he had never been conscripted into the US Army, in either a military or civilian capacity. In '43, they had rejected him as being of "unsound mind" after he told them in his interview that he could not guarantee that he would not die in spirit before dying in body and that he might feel the need, at any given moment, to sit cross-legged and recite verses from the Tao-Te-Ching, and , in '50, he was dismissed as a subversive and sent for psychiatric assessment for enquiring as to whether, rather than go to Korea, he could be sent to the Soviet Union as a healer with a remit to promote peace and love between capitalists and communists.

Arthur swore blindly that he and Srikanth had been together at Woodstock in August 1969, and he had witnessed Srikanth read Ravi Shankar's palm after his gig on the first day. Apparently, Srikanth had correctly predicted that Ravi would have a daughter who would play the sitar as well, if not better, than he did. Arthur and Srikanth travelled the States together and attended spiritual retreats. Often there would be extended periods of silence, in which groups meditated and ate together but would neither acknowledge nor look at each other, and Arthur reached states of heightened self-awareness that he never dreamed possible.

He would talk of sitting cross-legged for hours and the excruciating pain that would develop, particularly in his knees. He would "watch" the pain objectively, from outside his own body, and monitor the differing physical sensations that accompanied it. His body temperature would fluctuate wildly, even as he experienced throbbing or tingling or buzzing. With his eyes shut he would do a body scan by tracing a path from the top of his head to his toes or to his back. He became adept at pinpointing a tiny area, especially on his face, and then waiting for a sensation to happen.

Arthur viewed his life through the prism of the decade, and he liked to ascribe colors to these huge chunks of time. His thirties, a period of awakening and awe-inspiring discovery, were distinctly white in hue. His forties were his green period, reflecting both his naïve idealism and an early concern for the environment. Arthur had once been reprimanded and fined by the city council in San Francisco for digging up some paving stones in a public space and planting a row of apple trees. His fifties saw him afflicted by uncharacteristic bouts of hot-headed and impulsive behavior, one example being an altercation with a pet shop owner about a parrot, which was reported in the local paper. Redness permeated that particular segment of time.

His sixties heralded his melancholic blue period. Depressed at the onset of the Reagan years, Arthur retreated into his shell and spent huge amounts of time immersed in the Bible, the Koran, the Bhagavad Gita, and a myriad of other religious texts. The mother of all U-turns saw Arthur raise his profile to such an extent that, in his seventies, he became pretty in pink. Palm readings, group meditations, spiritual counseling, and impromptu street performances were the order of the day. So unburdened did he feel that he sometimes paraded around San Jose in nothing more than a thong. As his ninth decade unfolded, alongside the opening years of the twenty-first century, Arthur developed some altogether new traits. Indignation and irascibility, distinctly purple in character, and serenity and gentleness, decidedly yellow in tone, were juxtaposed. On the one hand, there would be frequent run-ins with café staff over the lack of froth on a cappuccino and suchlike and, on the other, there was his unique brand of welfare work. Arthur would take disadvantaged kids under his wing and impart to them nuggets of his twentieth century acquired wisdom. Teenagers who were undernourished and barely literate were taught how to palm read and could quote Khalil Gibran.

Shortly after turning seventy-three, sixty years after he'd left, Arthur returned to Tucson, for good. How he loved to rock gently back and forth in his hammock at night, wondering at the cosmic beauty of the star-laden canopy, all the while listening to the strange, bird-like clicking sound of the geckos, the yipping and yelping of coyotes in the adjacent wash and the exuberant chorus of the crickets. How he adored its subtle, undulating landscape, its understated hues, asparagus and olive green, sepia and russet brown. He often dreamt of gliding, free as a bird, through the dry desert air, caressing every cactus-laden contour, marveling at the majestic mesquite trees, drawn to its dusty, dried-out arroyos. He reveled in Tucson's retro signage, purred at its public art, especially its cornucopia of murals. He flirted ad infinitum with its fertile cultural scene and delighted in its demographic diversity. More than anything, he gloried in its gravitas. No Johnny-come-lately this place. Its ancestors tilled the soil four thousand years ago. There it sat, in all its raw, savage beauty, a bountiful basin carved into the Sonoran desert, straddling four eco-systems.

Every Saturday night, Arthur and his herpetologist friend, Fred, would hang out together. They'd smoke reefers and play scrabble, while listening to the Blues Review on KXCI. They both loved the folksy host, Marty Cool, who would give air time to musicians with wonderfully colorful names, such as Willie "big eye" Smith and Pine-Top Perkins and would urge listeners to go to gigs around town. "Tell'em Marty Cool sent ya, yes sir-ree," he would say, in his earthy southern drawl. Fred lived on a commune in Tucson's magical Dunbar Springs neighborhood, close to downtown. A sanctuary for all manner of creative types, environmentalists and activists, its tree-lined streets and yards were full of water harvesting tubes, solar panels, murals and assorted objects, some of which had been rescued from iconic old buildings. One such example was the huge lantern and neon sign of the "Ye Old Lantern" restaurant, both of which used to light up the night sky in magnificent fashion, as compelling as a still from a Disney movie.

Fred, whose house pets were a rattle snake and a Gila monster, would mesmerize Arthur with his encyclopedic knowledge of the local flora and fauna. Conversely, Arthur would dazzle Fred with the range of his talents. It had been eight years since Arthur read his palm and correctly predicted he would grow a fourteen inch ponytail.

Since the start of the noughties, as a British friend of his liked to refer to the opening decade of the twenty-first century, Arthur had been taking breakfast at Coffee Exchange on Campbell and Grant. A raspberry flavored Italian soda and two jam croissants were his standard fare. The Exchange was brim full of motley Tucson characters, who would while away many hours there. Bad Barry, an ageing hippy stoner whose sun bleached, leathery, torso resembled an overcooked pork chop, was one example. Another was Derrick the Devil, whose ability to demolish two dozen deviled eggs in the blink of an eye was legendary, not to mention the fact that he would store them in a furry pouch attached to his belt. Barry, Derrick, and Arthur could often be seen engaging in intense conversation, during which they regularly whispered into each other's ears.

Jackson was a young mathematics student who liked to shoot the breeze with Arthur now and again. Arthur had read his palm and confidently predicted that he would live a long, albeit impecunious life, marry a dark woman, and be contacted by his dead grandfather.

"Where the hell does he get that stuff? It's like ... I dunno, like he talks in riddles. I mean, is it crap or profound? Hell, I'm gonna ask him," Jackson said to his pals. He skipped across the floor to where Arthur was deeply absorbed in a tome on the Kabbala.

"Mr. Robertson, I hope you don't mind me asking, but I was wondering whether all that shit you come out with is, like, serious. Does it mean anything or are you just trying to confuse us with a load of old mumbo-jumbo?"

"My dear, fellow, let me assure you as amply as I can that I am no promulgator of platitudinous half-truths. I feel, therefore, I know. That is the basic and intuitive principle according to which I operate."

"Mr. R, are you messing with me again?"

"Jackson, men like you are the future of this country. I would not seek to engage in condescension or bitched up and bastardized behaviors."

"I'll take that as a no then, shall I?" Jackson was all smiles. He did not know whether to love or hate Arthur. But you could not ignore him and that was probably the point, thought Jackson.

Arthur spent his eighty-fourth birthday wishing he was dead. He had sunk very far, very fast, and wallowing around helplessly at the bottom of a squalid trough was a rare experience for him. He recalled one other extended bout of depression in the late '70s when he'd been on his back for months after a serious motorcycle accident. His precious Harley-Davidson M-65S had been totaled, and, a week later, a woman he'd fallen for ran off with Mad Dog DeGeneres, a minor Mafiosa from Vegas who had a penchant for biting off his victims' ears.

On this occasion, the trigger had been the loss of another prized possession. Arthur's apartment had been broken into, and his set of rare Japanese Tarot cards had been stolen. He'd bought them for seventy-five bucks in 1957 from a Japanese restauranteur, and they'd been pivotal in half a century of readings. "If I ever find the lowlife who's responsible for such egregious thievery I'll run him through with a sabre," said Arthur, lunging forward dramatically, fork in hand, to a somewhat bemused Mexican neighbor. He recalled the good old days in California when he never needed to lock his front door. How he lamented their passing.

He had no idea whether it was directly related to his deeply felt sadness or if it was simply a case of inevitable physical decline, but Arthur was then struck by incontinence for the very first time. Nasty business it was, too. Before long, he was engaged in a war of attrition with his own feces. To involuntarily fill up his pants with hot, steaming excreta made Arthur feel decidedly sub-human. At his lowest ebb, he'd often find himself naked, on all fours, sniffing his own shit. He would try desperately to clean it up but, more often than not, ended up smearing the stuff over the floors and walls. Several times, he passed out and had vivid dreams of being drowned by mounds of steaming horse dung. He woke up surrounded by dried lumps of his own fetid crap.

The doctor advised him to wear sanitary pads and do exercises to strengthen his rectum. Apparently, they involved tightening the rectal sphincter for several seconds at a time. If that didn't work, an electronic nerve stimulation device could be implanted into the rectum. As a last resort, an artificial anal sphincter could be introduced. What next? Arthur thought. Maybe I'll start pissing myself and need to have a state of the art, silver, alloy-coated catheter fitted.

It took three months, but Arthur managed to extricate himself from the mire. At one point, he really felt that he was on the way out, but his inner resilience had pulled him through. He proved to be adept at sphincter strengthening and was pleased to have added another skill to his repertoire. He'd certainly use it if he ever went on a spiritual retreat again.

It was around ten p.m. on a Monday night. Arthur was on the way home from an evening spent playing speed chess at the Coffee Exchange. In fact, it was the first time he'd left the house following his wretched period of depression. He would have been the first to admit he was looking unkempt. He was wearing workman's overalls because he had spent the whole day painting the living room. He was covered in paint, and there was a big red ketchup stain on his chest, the remnants of his quarter-pounder with jalapeños and chili peppers. Spicy was to

Arthur what honey was to a bee. He would have eaten curried cornflakes if given the chance. What looked like a mangled locust protruded out of his matted silver hair.

Arthur tucked his trousers into knee length green, purple, and white socks and set out on the short journey home. As he cycled north on Campbell towards Prince, his spindly legs rotated furiously. He passed The Blue Willow Restaurant and Gift Shop on his right, which, if his memory served him right, was named after a Chinese legend about two star-crossed lovers. The grub there was great, but it was rather too bourgeois for his liking. Arthur lived in a studio close to the Campbell Bridge, which spanned the Rillito Creek and housed a colony of Mexican free-tailed bats. He loved bats, did Arthur. As the only mammals capable of true and sustained flight and whose dung was used to make gunpowder in the American Civil War, he reckoned they did not get the recognition they deserved.

All of a sudden, a boy racer in a souped-up Golf GTI carved him up. Arthur honked his top of the range Wolo airsplitter dual tone horn with relish and gave him the middle finger. The Golf momentarily veered to the left as the surprised boy looked over his shoulder. "That'll teach you, you little upstart," Arthur chuckled to himself. But his mirth was cut short when the familiar refrain of a police siren drowned out the fading echo of his own.

"Do you know why I have stopped you, sir?"

"Probably because you're lonely and want to engage in earnest conversation with Baron Von Schlokmeister, the patron saint of mediocrity."

"Would you mind repeating that, sir?"

'Oh, don't worry yourself, young man. I'm just a poor, wayfaring stranger wandering through a land of woe. It's not personal.'

"Well, sir, I'm starting to take it personal, and I therefore suggest that you accompany me to the station. And as you don't seem to be aware of the reasons why I stopped you I'll tell you. You do not have a red reflector attached to the rear of the bicycle. It is illegal to operate a bicycle which has a siren attached to it, and you were cycling erratically. I suggest you attach your bike to that railing and then we'll head off in my vehicle."

"Young man, I do hope that this whole exercise doesn't turn out to be an anti-climax. I'm still recovering from a dose of the pox."

At the station on Miracle Mile Arthur was read his rights.

"You have the right to remain silent. Anything you say can and will be used against you in a court of law. You have the right to have an attorney present during questioning. If you cannot afford an attorney, one will be appointed for you. Do you understand these rights?"

"Silence is my preferred mode of communication. Why would I want to open my mouth and muddy the waters further?" said Arthur in a deliberately labored fashion. This stance was totally in keeping with his favorite mantra, which he loved to repeat and had for years been earmarked as his epitaph: he played the fool to keep the narrow, dull-witted, hateful and hidebound, self-serving, greedy, vulgar, and profane at bay.

The rookie looked bemused. "Er, so, Mr. Robertson, you do not require that to be repeated?"

"No, thank you, my friend. Economy is all. Repetition rarely serves us well."

"In that case, sir, we shall proceed to interview you under caution and provide you with an attorney."

"Proceed away, esteemed one, but I have no need of an attorney or any others who profit from the unlimited power of offended mediocrity."

As the interview progressed, Arthur maintained his air of insouciance, although, the truth was that he did not need to put on an act. He was carefree and had all the time in the world. They could drown him in a sea of bureaucracy if they so wished. Let them carry out their petty power-plays and their charade of procedural correctness, he thought. He felt no antagonism and did not seek to offend. It was simply the futility of it all that baffled him.

"Mr. Robertson, for the last time, if we release you will you give us an assurance that you will attach a red reflector to the rear of the bicycle and remove the siren without delay?"

"As I have indicated, young man, I would be happy to give you as many assurances as you require. However, within any document I sign I would like it noted that I, in turn, seek an assurance that you and your noble colleagues will, from now on, use all your best endeavors to rein in the wayward elements of this city's youth who persist in flouting common etiquette. I have an eight-point plan I would like you to consider."

"Sir, it seems that we will not be able to close this matter out tonight. I therefore have no option but to escort you to a cell where you will remain until we resume our interview in the morning."

"Escort away, young man."

As he sat crossed-legged on the concrete floor of the police department cell, Arthur found himself smiling as he contemplated the latest twist in his eighty-three-year odyssey on Planet Earth. He suddenly realized that he had broken new ground again. It was the first night he had ever spent in the police department cells in Arizona. To make the occasion extra special, he began to sing Elvis Presley's "Jailhouse Blues" out loud, while trying to summon up some yoga moves that he had not practiced for decades.

"You are free to go now, Mr. Robertson."

Arthur had spent a peaceful night meditating and writing poetry and was more than ready to resume his dialogue with Tucson's finest. "Go? Oh, kind sir, a magnanimous offer if ever I've heard one but a touch premature nonetheless."

"Sir?"

"Have you raised the question of my manifesto with your superiors?"

"Manifesto, sir?"

"Yes, the eight-point plan designed to bring to heel our misguided younger generation."

"No, sir. I thought you were just joshing me."

"Young man, I can assure you that where matters of such fundamental import are concerned, Arthur James Robertson Junior never jests."

"Okay, sir, do you have this plan in writing?"

"Of course it has been committed to the page. I'm no procrastinator, you know."

As Officer Krauthammer drove back to the station after dropping Arthur off at Coffee Exchange, he was feeling quite pleased with himself. He'd managed to appease the old boy by reassuring him that once the manifesto had been faxed to the station, he'd personally place it in front of Station Chief Laguerta. He'd given his word to Arthur, and they'd shaken hands on it. Anything to avoid a one-man occupation by a stubborn old mule who could talk his way out of a paper bag.

ARTHUR ROBERTSON'S 8-POINT PLAN TO RESCUE TUCSON'S YOUTH

To the youth:

1. Write down 6 goals for the day as soon as you wake up.
2. Seek out an old person. Do one thing for them and learn one thing from them.
3. Practice the 3 C's: Courtesy, Civility, and Community.
4. Spend one hour a day teaching yourself a skill such as drawing, painting, gardening, juggling, yo-yoing, dancing, and stilt-walking.

To the authorities:

5. Anti-Social Offender Sanctions (ASOS) to be introduced for infringements such as noise and environmental pollution or foul and abusive language.
6. Youth Curfew Orders (YCO) to be introduced for repeat offenders.
7. Rewards/incentive scheme to be introduced for responsible/selfless acts that benefit the community.
8. Regular youth forums to take place and the discussions publicized.

The above plan to be considered by representatives of Tucson's Law Enforcement, Legislators, and Youth.

Umm, obviously an eccentric old bird, thought Chief Laguerta after Krauthammer had passed Arthur's manifesto onto him, but there's some quite interesting stuff in here. Think I'll show it to Congresswoman Jefferson at our next meeting.

No Way Out

Luis Salcido, a modest Mexican bookkeeper, had been offered the world by Raul Gonzales, a hubristic Mexican businessman. Twenty thousand bucks a year more than he was currently earning plus perks—one such enticement being a ten day sojourn every year at Gonzales's villa in Puerto Peñasco, a burgeoning resort town on the northern tip of Mexico's Sea of Cortez, known to Americans as Rocky Point—was more than tempting. In fact, in view of the miserable situation in which Luis found himself, it was simply too good to turn down. His wife, Lupita, had been diagnosed with a rare blood disorder and would need extensive treatment. Their insurance policy was good for fifty thousand but the doctors had estimated that the cost could run to as much as a hundred thousand. As it was, they were going to have to mortgage all the remaining equity in their adobe house in Barrio Viejo.

Luis had known Gonzales for three years. They'd been introduced by the pastor of the church they both attended, for whom Luis did the books and Gonzales paid for the refurbishment. The latter man was heralded within the Hispanic community for his philanthropy and regularly appeared, as happy as a clam, on the society pages of Tucson's Spanish language weekly, *La Estrella*. A charismatic, six foot two, square-jawed beanpole of a man with a vise-like handshake that had been known to inflict extensive soft tissue damage, he always made an impression. Conversely, Luis was eminently forgettable: softly spoken, five feet nothing, with an average build, no defining features, and a blotchy complexion. Observant types occasionally noticed that his right eye was a darker green than his left, but, that aside, Luis never received any comments about his appearance.

The exuuberant Gonzales had immediately identified the timid Luis as a safe pair of hands. Within a month, Luis had served out his notice period at Wickhams Self-Storage, where he'd worked for eleven straight years and was ensconced behind his tobacco-lacquered oak desk in a huge, rammed earth hall at Gonzales Industries. Luis was very pleased to be working out of Menlo Park. He could sit at his desk and see Sentinel Peak, commonly known as "A Mountain." Gonzales liked the idea that the Hohokam Indians lived on the site in the 1300s. "Those guys were awesome. They were already creating sophisticated rainfall runoff systems. Sucks that they died out like that. Nobody knows for sure what happened. I think they got flooded out."

As was the case every Monday night, Luis and his childhood friend, David Goddard, were drinking *cervezas* at Sir Veza's on Speedway and Swan. They were sitting on the outside terrace from where they could drool like slavering puppy dogs every time a classic car passed by. What Luis and David didn't know about classic cars wasn't worth knowing. Neither of them ever lost an opportunity to disappear into their respective garages where they would lose themselves for hours on end in a cornucopia of leather bound seats and custom door panels, chrome alloy shift knobs, and gleaming metallic fins and fenders. Their love affair with the motorcar had begun in their late teens when the pair had driven all the way up the west coast of California in a white 1953 Chevy Corvette convertible.

The boys had had much in common. Both were travelling without adult supervision for the first time. Both were virgins. Both had overprotective mothers and disciplinarian fathers. And both were rather fragile, physically and mentally. Luis, a late developer who hadn't reached puberty until he turned seventeen, was teased mercilessly by his peers who labeled him "shorty Salcido." Too shy to interact with girls, he endured a painful adolescence. As for David, he suffered from severe acne throughout his teenage years. As if that wasn't enough, he was afflicted by a nervous tic such that every minute or so he'd puff out his cheeks as though he were blowing an imaginary trumpet.

"So what does Gonzales want you to do, Luis?"

"*La cocinera mi amigo*, a little bit of cooking."

"Say what, Luis?"

"He wants me to cook the books, David. Plain and simple."

"Jesus, Luis. That is not smart. I take it you'll give that shit a wide berth."

"I wish it was that easy. The thing is I need this gig. I really do. It's a minefield, but it's the only option I've got right now."

"You got options, bro. I'm sure if we arranged a fundraiser you could raise a decent amount of money."

"I can't do that, Dave. I'm a proud man. I just can't go around with a begging bowl. I would never be able to look anyone in the eye again."

"Luis, it's madness. You could end up behind bars."

"I know, es *una locura*—total madness—*pero*, if it saves Lupita's life then it's a price worth paying. *Ojala,* it will never come to that."

"He's a piece of work, that Gonzales. Ruthless son of a gun. I'd love to see that guy get his comeuppance."

"I know, I know. He's not for real. But I can play him, too. It's a two-way street, Dave."

"Do you think you can pull it off, Luis?"

"*Si, es un* cakewalk, *mi amigo*. I'll cover my fat ass, you can bet on that."

David and Luis watched as a tall young girl wearing Ray-bans, flip-flops, and a tight-fitting beige miniskirt sat down opposite them. She crossed her long, veiny legs and began to read *Cosmopolitan*. Her dainty feet were perfectly manicured and her nails were painted green.

"See that, Dave. Her nails are the same color as my Buick. How about that?" said Luis, genuinely excited.

"Good spot, buddy. Maybe you can persuade her to test drive it when you're done working your magic?"

"Ha ha, ever the wit, aren't you, Goddard? Perhaps she'll let me brush up her bodywork at the same time." Luis let rip with a deep throaty laugh that sounded like a stuttering car exhaust.

A tanned, muscular guy in a Wildcats sleeveless T-shirt sat down right next to the girl. He had tightly permed hair and some tufts of fluffier hair sprouting from underneath his bottom lip. Luis pictured their naked bodies locked together, her pale, silken legs coiled around the broad expanse of his tanned back. An image of vanilla streaked coffee ice cream entered his mind. It was far easier for him to envisage others making love. He himself had not done so for over six years, and he no longer saw himself as a sexual being. His inactivity didn't bother him unduly; it was just something he'd fallen out of the habit of doing.

He was in no doubt that when the time was right he and Lupita would resume conjugal relations. After all, they were still very much in love after twenty-two years of marriage. In the age of immediate gratification and grasping rapacity, Luis was a rarity. He was the one-paced hedgehog who bided his time and rarely departed from his tried and trusted routines.

Luis was sitting opposite Gonzales, who was on his cell phone. He had stubby fingers and his nails were at least a quarter of an inch long. Very creepy, he was thinking when Gonzales finished his conversation with the words "no later than Tuesday midnight, understood?" He leaned forward, smiled devilishly and said to Luis, "So, my little genius, are we plotting a crafty course?"

"Raúl, if only that was true. I'm a Steady Eddy. I get the job done and that's about it."

"*Exactamente*, Luis. That's why I hired you. It's all about stepping up to the plate and seeing it through. You wouldn't believe the amount of flakes who've jerked me around in the last few years." They ran through the four-point plan for the umpteenth time. 1) Luis would buy a company off the shelf, and it would be a wholly-owned subsidiary of Las Palmas Leisure, Inc., which was gearing up to tender for a new Leisure Center downtown. It would be part of the second phase of the downtown Rio Nuevo development. Gonzales was already in negotiations with a South Korean investor. 2) Half of the current debt of Las Palmas would be moved off the books and into the new subsidiary, thereby rendering the latest profit and loss accounts for Las Palmas a good deal healthier. 3) Half of the costs of land surveys, development consultants' fees, and investment in machinery relating to Rio Nuevo would be recorded in the accounts of the new subsidiary. 4) The costs outlined in number three that pertained to Las Palmas would be spread out over a six-month period as far as the accounts were concerned.

The South Korean guy was coming to Tucson, and Luis would be expected to run through all the figures with him and address any concerns he may have.

Luis and David were enjoying a reunion with a bunch of old school friends at Mi Nidito Mexican Restaurant on South 4th Avenue, an establishment that had been feeding Tucsonans for sixty years and conjured up so many memories for the Latino community in particular. Indeed, it was Luis's sole claim to fame that he'd met Bill Clinton there in 1999. Well lubricated, he recounted the anecdote for the eighty-eighth time. Apparently, Luis had been waiting in line for over an hour when the president was ushered in and became the first person in years who didn't have to wait for a table. Luis swore blind that he was having a pee when Clinton came in and used the adjacent urinal. Luis asked the president if he liked the food, and Clinton replied, "It's awesome. I am fucking stuffed. Definitely gonna need to run this off tomorrow."

The others all followed on with anecdotes of their own. Nobody cared that they repeated these same stories year after year. Javier, a chunky firefighter, whose nickname was "El Intrepido"—"The Fearless One"—reminded everyone that in 1991, during the monsoon season, he'd been a guest at a *Quinceañera* celebration at the legendary El Casino Ballroom, a few blocks north of Mi Nidito, when half the roof blew off. He saw an empty Cadillac that had been speared through the windshield and then through the driver's seat. Javier also derived vicarious pride because his dad had seen Fats Domino and Little Richard in concert there, way back when—the sixties, he thought.

"Hey guys, do you remember that time we did a Chinese fire drill at the lights at 44th and 6th 'cos we wanted to make those girls standing on the sidewalk laugh? And JJ gives them a moony in the process, falls down, and we drive off without him. And when we get back a few minutes later he's been cited by a cop for lewd behavior," said David. They all howled with laughter. "Fuck that was funny. Those girls were loving it. One of them said to me, 'Hey, when that guy's finished having his ass slapped by the cops send him over here and we'll give him a proper spanking.' JJ was seriously tempted. Only thing was the broad turned out not to be a broad, but JJ was so shitfaced he still considered it for a while."

"Crazy fuck. God rest his soul," said Ernesto. They all raised a glass to JJ who had succumbed to Leukemia at the age of twenty-nine.

Don't worry, *mi ángel*, we will come through this ordeal as good as new. *Nuestro Dios* has, in his wisdom, decided that we must be challenged. Well, so be it. We are strong. We will prevail."

"*Mi amor*. I'm scared. I'm not ready to die. If I'm not here who will cook your favorite chicken fajitas? Who will polish your shoes? Who will massage your bad ankle? *Ay ay ay*. It's not fair." Lupita rested her head on Luis's shoulder and sobbed gently. It was the night before her first major surgery, and they were both feeling emotional. He'd always been her whole world. Unassuming, unflappable, even-tempered, sensitive, and as honest as the day is long, for her, he was as near to perfection as it was possible for a human being to be. And in his eyes, Lupita was all that he'd ever dreamed of in a woman: pure, gentle, affectionate, reliable, accepting, and modest. They had never so much as had a cross word, something others found freaky and boring. The only time there had been even a hint of discord between them was when he beat her at gin rummy seven times in a row, and she questioned him as to whether he'd been secretly taking lessons from a pro.

"*Mi vida*. It's not your time to go. Trust me. Don't forget, we still have to visit your brother in Acapulco. And we also need to do the Santiago de Compostela pilgrimage. We have so much more to experience together, *mi guapissima*." And we have to resume our lovemaking, Luis thought. If that happened it would symbolize a true renaissance in our lives, the opening of a glorious new chapter.

"Luis Salcido, *estás un rock-star*. Kwon loves you. According to him, nobody ever explained profit and loss, balance sheets, and income projections as well as you. When Las Palmas is up and running he wants us to go to Seoul to visit him. It would be fantastic, no?" Gonzales didn't wait for Luis's response. He was already inserting into the computer the CD containing the architect's plans and mock-ups. "*Mira*, these will blow you away. We've got a skating rink and a wave park, as well as a gymnasium, saunas, spas, and steam rooms—you know, all the usual stuff. Those twelve hundred University of Arizona students who are being accommodated along the new streetcar route are going to be all over Las Palmas. That reminds me, I need to contact those university honchos to see if they want a bunch of memberships at a discounted rate. Those academics like their perks, Luis. You'd be surprised."

Gonzales's enthusiasm was infectious, and he soon had Luis hooked on the scheme and chipping in with suggestions. "Have you thought about handball and racquetball courts? There's always demand for them. Oh, and you might want to think about a space for roller derby—that's a booming sport."

Gonzales was suitably impressed and offered to treat Luis to dinner at Blue

Fin, his favorite fish restaurant in town. "Have you ever been there? The lobster is *maravillosa.*"

Casas Adobes Plaza, variously described as "an Old World lifestyle plaza," or "an elegant, upscale, outdoor shopping center," was exactly the kind of place Luis felt uncomfortable in. As he looked around, what he mostly discerned was pretentiousness and vanity. Gonzales, on the other hand, was in his element. Anywhere you could see and be seen by the moneyed class was grist to his mill. Luis soon understood that Gonzales made a point of establishing at least one new contact wherever he went. On the night they dined together at Blue Fin, he made a beeline for a very classy, middle-aged woman who was dressed in a cream trouser suit and was wearing very long, spectacular, teardrop-shaped, pink diamond earrings. Luis watched him as he schmoozed her and keyed her number into his cellphone.

"Smart lady, she's got oodles of experience in the arts and entertainment industry. Semi-retired, does an occasional gig as a docent at the Tucson Museum of Art. Just what I need to front up Las Palmas. Let's see if I can't make it worth her while to come out of retirement." Back at their table, Gonzales, glint in his eye, eased back into his seat and ran the palm of his hand across his chest and stomach. He does that quite a lot, thought Luis. As they sipped their coffees, Gonzales said, "Oh, Luis, I almost forgot. I need you to work your magic on the accounts for a carwash I own in San Diego. I've got some external funds I want to absorb into the business. It's a little bit naughty—*pero* nothing you can't handle."

Luis felt a pang in the pit of his stomach. This was it. Just what he'd always feared would happen with Gonzales. It was one thing to be a little bit creative with the accounts, but this was a wholly different kettle of fish. It was money laundering, pure and simple. "Raúl, are you sure about this? It sounds risky to me. It's the kind of thing the IRS will pounce on."

"Luis, I didn't realize that you were such a little worrier. Don't sweat it, amigo. It's nothing significant, trust me. Only twenty, twenty-five k and it only happens once in a blue moon. Almost impossible to detect, believe me." He leaned forward and patted Luis on the shoulder. And then he was gone. Discussion over.

"You look worried, Luis. What's going on, friend? It's not Lupita, is it?" enquired David.

"No, *gracias a Dios*, she's doing good. The op went very well. No, it's Gonzales, of course. Exactly what I predicted would happen." Luis looked glum. He tugged at his left ear lobe, something he always did when he was worried.

"Why, what's he done?"

"It's not anything he's actually done. It's what he wants me to do. I thought it was all too good to be true at Gonzales Holdings."

"Luis, would you mind just telling me what the problem is."

"Yes, yes, I'm sorry. I'm a little distracted. He wants me to do some money laundering. He's hiding a chunk of dirty money in a carwash business he owns in San Diego, and I have to do the accounts. Fuck it, man."

"What an ass! Hardly a surprise though, Luis. Do you think you can disguise it? How dangerous is it?"

"I'm not that worried about this one. It's not a huge amount, and it's very unlikely to attract attention. But it's so obviously going to be the tip of the iceberg. People like Gonzales never know when to stop and they feel untouchable. And I'm in it up to my neck now. There's no going back." Luis shook his head ruefully and brushed some specks of dandruff off his shoulder.

"Luis, I know it's not ideal, buddy, but you're going to have to run with it and accept it as your reality. You knew what you were getting into with this Gonzales character, right?"

"I know, Dave, I know. You're right. I just have to back myself to cover all the bases. I must hold my nerve. Whatever curve balls come my way will be returned with interest."

"Ataboy. That's the Luis I know and love." David loved the little fella like a brother. He was the only thing in his life that was more reliable than the V8 engine in his Range Rover Classic, which had started first time for the last seventeen years. He knew for a fact that without Luis he wouldn't be alive. The man had saved his life, for God's sake. Not once, but twice. Seven or eight years ago, they'd been on the I-10 just outside Tucson, on the way back from a classic car convention in Phoenix. David had fallen asleep at the wheel. Luis had reacted like greased lightning, grabbing the wheel and nudging David awake. When they had been teenagers, they were kayaking and their boat overturned. David hit his head against a rock and lost consciousness. In the nick of time, Luis had grabbed hold of his ankle as he started drifting away. With great difficulty, he'd held him above water until help arrived.

Luis told David all about Las Palmas, and he agreed it sounded exciting. However, given the history of Rio Nuevo—millions spent on consultants but next to nothing to show for it –David doubted it would ever see the light of day. "Luis, as it stands now, it's a two hundred thirty million black hole which the FBI's investigating. Plus, the new Rio Nuevo Board that runs the show and the city council are already at each other's throats. It's hard to see how it moves forward from here."

"I accept there have been major problems, Dave, but it does appear to me that the wheels are finally turning. There's proper accountability now and plenty of building work happening. Don't forget the El Mercado de San Agustín development, close to my office, is part of Rio Nuevo, plus the Fox and Rialto Theater renovations. And there's also the modern streetcar and the Martin Luther King public housing project. Tucson can still become the Athens of the Southwest. We've got to keep living the dream, buddy."

"Dunno, Luis. Maybe Tucson should just concentrate on being Tucson instead of trying to ape San Francisco. The folks running this place seem to mess everything up. I mean, look at the way they let all the spring training die out. The Rockies and the Diamondbacks were never going to stay at Tucson Electric Park. If they'd built a sexy new facility closer to downtown we might have had a chance."

Luis took the plunge and did what he had to do for Gonzales. He could see the funny side of the way Gonzales always managed to come up with a new adjective to describe whatever task he assigned to him: from naughty to creative to subtle to radical to enterprising to bold to dynamic to clever to artful. The list was endless, as was the parallel list that Luis employed to characterize his own position in relation to Gonzales: from hooked to tied to bound to chained to shackled to tethered to fastened. The unpalatable fact was that he was no longer an autonomous person. Gonzales pretty much owned him. He had effectively become his PA and had to make himself available twenty-four-seven, and it was certainly rare for him to go even twelve hours without a phone call from this behemoth who Luis felt could toy with him like King Kong holding a human miniature in the palm of his hand.

But he was earning more money than he'd ever earned before, and that was, after all, why he'd taken the job in the first place. The medical bills were coming in thick and fast and being able to cover them was crucially important for

Luis. Lupita was responding well to the treatment, and he was hopeful that she would soon be well enough to recuperate for a week or two down at Rocky Point.

As Luis drove home from the office one night, deep in thought, he hit a red at the corner of Congress and Grande. He noticed that the crumbling, fading old mural of the *Virgen de Guadalupe* on the side wall of what used to be Menlo Park Video had been repainted. Now a barbershop, it was all green and red and shiny and the word: "VIDEOS," which had appeared in huge lettering, was gone. Luis felt sad. The ironic juxtaposition of an advertisement with religious iconography had been what made that mural so special. "I loved that mural," Luis said to himself. It said so much about Latinos in the modern world. Catholicism and capitalism. The ultimate synergy. Not a new concept but a very Hispanic way of expressing it. Buy a video, say a prayer. All bases covered. Purity maintained.

When Gonzales didn't call with some instruction or other—collect this, copy that, launder the other, be it a business or a suit—Luis immediately felt queasy. In the year that he'd been working for the man it had never happened before. After forty-eight hours, Luis called his cell phone and land line but got no reply from either. He tried one or two of his business acquaintances but they knew nothing. He went to his house but there was no one there. Something could have happened to him, health-wise, but Luis doubted that because he would have heard something from the community. In all likelihood, he'd taken the family across the border and was lying low. Someone like Gonzales would inevitably have to spend periods of time under the radar.

Luis was sure he'd receive a call from him within the week. But *nada*. A week became two became three and then it was a month. Luis checked his bank account and his salary had come through as normal. Jesus, what the hell! Luis didn't know what to think anymore. He was very fearful and expected his house to be raided any minute by the IRS. Was this it? Had the whole edifice come tumbling down? Was his time as a free man about to end? But there was nothing whatsoever he could do. Reporting him missing was out of the question.

For the next two months, Luis went to work as normal and juggled Gonzales' affairs as best he could. But the funds in the one company bank account that he had access to dwindled to nothing, and the handful of issues he'd been attending to resolved themselves. Then the police turned up at Luis's house. When he opened the door and saw them he nearly died. He needn't have worried. The neighbors had reported the family missing. The kids hadn't been to school. Gonzales had missed a Hispanic business event at which he'd been due to speak. All the funds had been withdrawn from the wife's bank account. Did Luis know anything? He told them he was just as much in the dark as everyone else. Did he have any ideas as to why this man and his family would disappear? No. it was completely out of character. Gonzales was a successful businessman and a well-respected figure within the Hispanic community.

When his salary was stopped after the third month Luis understood Gonzales had meant to make sure he'd be taken care of for the first three months. He appreciated the fact that Gonzales had left him in the dark. Involving him would only have brought problems. He was interviewed twice by the police, but it was all routine stuff. No mention was ever made of tax or financial wrongdoing. The calm before the storm? Possibly. But maybe he and Gonzales really had been a Class A double act—as airtight as Apollo 11. Luis liked to think so.

Gonzales had been missing for a year. Luis had taken two part-time bookkeeping jobs, one for a firm of plumbers and the other for a bedding company. Once again, drab uniformity was the order of the day. Luis was in his element and had slotted seamlessly back into the old routine. As he looked back on his eighteen month stint with Gonzales it seemed more and more like a dream. And yet, a part of him actually missed the loveable old rogue. True, he'd never been comfortable with the large element of unpredictability, and the unwilling incursion into criminality had weighed heavily on him. And he would always have to live with the possibility that it might yet come back to bite him. But there was no doubt, Gonzales had style and charisma and had always treated Luis impeccably. He'd never met anyone quite like him, and he was fairly certain that he never would again.

He had no clue why Gonzales had melted into the ether, but he believed he was alive and living somewhere in South or Central America, most likely under a new identity. He was sure he'd never see or hear from him again. The man had entered his life at exactly the right moment. The pair of them would toast and say a prayer for him every month. For Luis, the specter of Gonzales would always loom large.

Red Tag To A Bull

"Yeh, well, you just gotta pop a cap in someone's ass now and again, know what I'm saying, man?" said John Wilkerson. John had always been fiercely loyal to his brother and now, as Brady faced a possible seven or eight years in the can for shooting his neighbor, William Anderson, in the ankle, was no different. That did not mean, however, that he was not deeply pissed off at his brother's act of rank stupidity.

"That may be so, my friend, but, hell, the guy didn't run off with his woman or something. He got him another red tag. Irritating, for sure, very irritating, in fact, but hardly worth pumping him full of lead for that." Aaron was the Wilkerson brothers' lifelong friend and, so often, the voice of reason that kept them on the right side of the tracks. He often wondered why he remained so loyal to them because they never expressed any gratitude. He figured it was habit more than anything. Either that or the fact that worrying about their lives meant that he did not have to worry about his own. Now, though, he was pretty much at the end of his tether. Brady was a hothead who never learnt from his mistakes. He'd shot his neighbor for no good reason, and that was a bridge too far in Aaron's eyes. As for John, his views had become increasingly objectionable since joining the Tea Party crew, and Aaron had begun to feel uncomfortable in his presence. Or maybe John had always held those views but just felt more comfortable or confident about expressing them.

The Wilkerson brothers and Aaron Hamilton had lived in the Old Pueblo since they were five, six and eight years old respectively, and they'd been near neighbors for some twenty-two years. Aaron was an only child and lived with his mother in a trailer on a retirement park at Flowing Wells, a scruffy neighborhood in Northwest Tucson. The Wilkerson family house, with its distinctive red lava rock gravel, was a few blocks away. The neighborhood was dotted with car repair garages, mobile food units, and dive bars. There was an abundance of urban detritus: abandoned mattresses, sofas, televisions, and even the odd bath tub. Smoke belched from the mesquite grills of hot dog and seafood taco stands, and sinister dust devils enabled the spirits of the underworld to float on the hot, heavy air.

"I dunno, bro. I know I'm a bad motherfucker all the way round, but that guy's been on my case for far too long. He's had it coming. I just cracked. I hate that guy's cocky attitude". Even as he heard himself speak, Brady knew that this time his bravado would count for nothing. He'd overstepped the mark and would have to pay the price. He felt nauseous as he imagined himself in the clink in a triple bunk bed situation again. Three years ago, after he'd been convicted of assault, he'd had above him a Russian ex-weightlifter, who brushed his teeth with vodka, and below him, a limp-wristed, close-talking, Chicago dockworker.

"Listen, Brady, you don't deserve it, but I was chit-chatting with this very smart lawyer guy, and he thinks he may be able to cut down the sentence," said Aaron. But I'll tell you what, dude, this is the last time I put myself out for you. You got that into your thick skull?"

"Yes, Aaron, I got it firmly situated in my thick skull. Now what's the dealio?"

"Well, this guy, Coogan, I think he said his name was, reckons there may be mitigating circumstances on account of your history with Anderson and him entering your house without consent, seizing your property." Anderson had made off with two of Brady's plant pots which, wrongly believing them to be cannabis plants, he'd then turned into the police.

'Exactly, man, enough was enough. That asshole has been on my case for far too long." Brady's saliva frothed up at either side of his lips, as it tended to do when he got over-excited. "You really came up trumps this time, Hamilton. When this is all over I swear to God I'm gonna take you...."

"You're getting carried away again, Brady. There are no guarantees. I'm just telling you what the man said. I still need to persuade him to take you on."

People who met Coogan never forgot him. A mere five foot two inches tall, barrel-chested, but with an impossibly flat butt, a mop of wavy grey hair, and piercing, marble green eyes, he was a physical magnet. And the force of his personality was equally irresistible. He would breeze into a room, silvery tongue at the ready. "Ok folks. What we have here is a situation that calls for the agility of a cheetah, the cunning of a fox, the patience and discipline of a nun on heat, and the brass balls of a Vietnam Vet with an attitude, i.e. me. *Capiche capula?*"

As far as Coogan was concerned, it wasn't rocket science. You always needed an edge over your opponent, and he would move hell or high water to find one. If you gave a situation enough thought there was always something to be teased out. There had been one case in which the only thing a victim of a mugging had remembered was that the guy who stabbed and robbed him had silver in his teeth which had been glinting in the sun. Of course, the attacker might have had dental fillings but Coogan had a hunch that what the victim described might just have been the key to solving the crime. He repeatedly asked folks if they remembered seeing anyone who had silver in his mouth. Three years later, he was chit-chatting with a jailbird he'd been interviewing about a sexual assault, and the guy happened to mention that his ex-cellmate, who was a career criminal, had a penchant for chewing on can pull-tabs. Coogan knew instantly that he'd found his man. He followed up and, sure enough, a DNA test linked the man to his mugging case.

As far as Brady's case was concerned, Coogan felt that Anderson's history of harassing Brady and other neighbors, taken together with the events on the night in question, gave him enough ammunition. It would depend on the judge being amenable to their initial, pre-hearing arguments around mitigation, but he was fairly confident on that score. Worst case scenario, Brady goes away for around seven years, but Coogan reckoned he could cut that in half.

"Let's subpoena the guy's ass for a deposition. The dirty rat." Coogan had the bit between his teeth again. He was on one of his legendary rolls. There was no one better at weeding out witnesses, especially recalcitrant ones who had no conception of performing a civic duty. Many a drifter, inmate, drug-pusher, and pimp had been on the receiving end of a "Coogan catch." Almost everyone with an interest in the law in Tucson knew this term. It had become an integral part of the city's legal lexicon.

On this occasion, the reluctant witness was a guy called Gilbert, a former neighbor of Anderson's who'd been involved in several altercations with him and had first-hand evidence that he had a problem controlling his temper. Apparently, Anderson had reported him to the city council for not cutting his grass and weeds to within the permitted height, and he'd also accused him of stealing his blue recycling bin and illegally keeping chipmunks and raccoons as pets. Basically, he wouldn't give the guy a minute's peace. Eventually, Gilbert got so pissed off that he sought legal advice and took Anderson to court on grounds of harassment. Anderson refused to back down and argued that Gilbert had been willfully negligent and irresponsible. The judge laughed him out of court and issued an injunction against harassment, prohibiting Anderson from going within two hundred feet of Gilbert or his home.

Coogan was at The Meat Rack, a dive bar whose motto was "Liquor Where She Likes It." It was run by Jim Anderson, nicknamed God, a legendary figure in Tucson who claimed to have branded over twelve hundred customers in his own rugged, bald-headed, image. In return, the branded ones got fifty-percent off food and drinks for life. Aside from the multiple panties and bras hanging from the ceiling and the picture of a young Arnold Schwarzenegger with his finger inserted in a woman's vagina, the weirdest thing in the bar was a sex room containing restraints and sex-toys. The erotic effigy of an anteater with a remote-controlled dildo was possibly the oddest one of all.

Coogan had been tipped off that Gilbert hung out there. He wasn't around but a guy who absent-mindedly tore a hamburger to shreds with his hands as he spoke, gave Coogan an approximate address for Gilbert. As he stepped out onto the sidewalk, there were a couple of bare-chested tweekers in front of him. They were grappling with each other and shouting. Their words were so slurred he couldn't follow anything they were saying. One of them had such a blackened face it looked like he'd just emerged from a coal mine. He was sweating profusely and his eyes were darting all over the place. The other one was very twitchy and covered in pimples. On the ground was a flashlight. Hmm, they look familiar. I wonder if they're the ones living in the wash next to Albertsons on Speedway and Silverbell who I visited a couple of years back, thought Coogan, as he slid into his Jeep and headed for the street where the elusive Gilbert might be.

"So, I got you bail, Brady, because they don't consider you a flight risk. But for fuck's sake stay out of trouble. okay?"

"Okay, Mr. Coogan, you got it."

"Tell me something, Brady, why did you do it?"

"Good question, Mr. Coogan. That's something I've been asking myself ever since that night. I know I got a bad temper, but it wasn't really anger this time. I just wanted to teach that loser a lesson. Words don't work with him. It's been going on for years. But obviously it was a bad move, and I'm gonna pay for it big time."

"Sadly, that's true. You will again be deprived of your liberty, and I urge you to use the time you are going to have on your hands to think long and hard about what you want to do with your life, because if you carry on like this there's only going to be one outcome."

"I know, Mr. Coogan, you're so right. I want to put things right. Believe me, I do."

"Oh, by the way, some good news. I've managed, finally, to get a hold of Gilbert. His statement will be very useful. Bit of a whacko though, found him racing hamsters on his porch."

John Wilkerson's first wife had left him for another woman, something he would never get over. The idea that a dike could satisfy her but he couldn't made him feel sick. And now it was okay for them to be out and proud in the military. Jesus, how the hell was America going to defend itself when the front lines were populated by queers? He'd heard liberals saying sexuality made no difference to fighting ability, but he knew that was a load of bull. A friend of his who'd fought in the first Gulf War swore blind that a gay had hit on him in the showers, and because he'd reacted violently, the gay bore a grudge against him. Apparently, the guy was so reckless in a combat situation it nearly cost them their lives.

John and Aaron were shooting pool at Old Chicago on Campbell. John, thickset and edgy, leant over the pool table, his ample midriff encroaching onto the green baize like an onrushing wave. One of the stud buttons on his tight-fitting denim shirt popped open, releasing a blob of whiter than white never seen the sun flesh that closely resembled rice pudding. He smirked and nodded towards one of the flat-screen TVs that was showing a match at the soccer world cup. "At least the Italians all look like Italians. The French, they're mainly African, right? And those Ghana players, they sure are fast, but, to me, they all look like lion tamers."

"Wait a minute, John. Lion tamers? What the fuck? That sounds racist to me. What's gotten into you? The other day it was gay folks and now this."

"Don't be silly, Aaron. You know me better than that. I'm just saying stuff, okay? It don't mean shit. You know I'm not a racialist. You saw me last week with that Black chick, right? Ease up, bro. You take stuff so serious these days. Your liberal chums been getting to you or what?"

"No, no one's been getting to me. I just don't like some of the crap you come out with these days."

Aaron was heading towards the rest room when he heard John's final riposte. "Live and let live, Aaron. Whatever happened to my First Amendment rights?"

The truth was that John believed every single word that had just come out of his mouth. And it was a big enough sacrifice for him to deny it if anyone called him a racist. The fucking politically correct society that he believed we now lived in made him puke. He looked back fondly on the pre-civil rights era. He was all over Rand Paul, who'd questioned the application of the Civil Rights Act in the private sector, and he got off on the thought that when Palin, Bachmann, and Company took over on Capitol Hill he'd be able to own a bar and ban Negroes and gays. And as for those prima donna soccer players, he hated the way they acted up like a bunch of women. "You'd have to barbecue me on a meat rack before I rolled around on the ground like that" was one of his favorite lines.

Aaron was kicking back with his neighbor, Chuck, a paper-thin long distance truck driver, whose penchant for oatmeal and granola bars made him an object of ridicule among his fellow, carnivorous truckers. The eerily quiet retirement park they lived in could easily have featured on the pages of a children's book. It was littered with dainty little ornamentals, anything from ducks, rabbits, and zebras to Indians, knights in armor, and pagodas.

The two of them were working their way through a twelve-pack of Dos Equis, alongside the attractive tree and tubular marsh grass lined lake. The radio was on in the background. Alice Cooper was doing his show on KLPX. He played great rock music but appeared to become more eccentric by the week, referring to himself as "the sultan of sick, the queen of the damned, and all the other shit," and coming out with all manner of random things like "If you haven't played enough Led Zep, an inspector will hit you in the face with a herring," and "Is this the week you are finally diagnosed with leprosy?" Chuck, who was wearing knee-high black socks, black slippers, a wife-beater, and a necklace with a chunky silver cross, was saying how lucky they were to live where they did. "Did you know Flowing Wells was given an All-American City Award in 2007? It's only given to ten communities in the country every year you know. We oughta be proud of that."

"Guess so, but I'd rather be living some place where the average age wasn't seventy-three," replied Aaron, who, as his Alzheimer afflicted mother's sole caregiver, was somewhat tied down. Aaron had long felt dissatisfied with his life. He was bright, nice looking—slim, straight, jet-black hair, tanned skin—and had no real money worries but had always been shackled by his family circumstances. An adopted only child, his parents were already in their sixties by the time he reached his teens. Pretty much from the age of twenty he'd cared for both of them and, for the last seven years, just his mother. Only twice in his life had he ever been able to get away for more than a week and, even then, he'd had to spend hours on the phone with doctors and pharmacists. At the very moment he was losing his virginity his father had called the hotel room.

Anderson was an angry man. He was forever engaged in running battles with people in his neighborhood. He was proud of his house—the only one in the street to have state-of-the-art louvered vinyl shutters—and always made sure that it was in pristine condition, inside and out. And he firmly believed in old-fashioned civility and social etiquette. When those living around him failed to live up to what he perceived to be his own high standards, it irritated him no end. Loud music, parties, the smell of marijuana drifting across his backyard, overflowing trash bins or trash bins which were left curbside all week, overgrown weeds, peeling paint, damaged fencing, dumping unwanted items on the sidewalk—Anderson could not abide any of these things and he never let anything go. More often than not he was a man on a mission. No wonder he was known as "The Rottweiler." All he wanted was for folks to have some respect, both for themselves and for others. Was that too much to ask for? Apparently so.

He made it his business to know every City of Tucson ordinance, everything

from the permitted height for lawn grass—six inches—and weeds—ten inches—
to the rule about when trash bins had to be removed from the curbside after
collection—same day—to the criteria relating to noise pollution—the sound
amplification system in a vehicle or the sound and vibration must not be clearly
audible at a distance of fifty feet. He'd been responsible for at least six houses
in the neighborhood receiving red tags, notices the police stick on what are
considered disorderly houses, in which a gathering of five or more people are
causing excessive noise, littering, obstructing the street, drinking in public,
and generally disturbing the peace. The tag remained for one hundred eighty
days and an immediate fine of a hundred dollars was levied. Brady had been the
recipient of two of the six notices.

"Brady, there's a guy at the front door complaining about the music."

Brady was in the bathroom doing a line of coke. "Is he small with a Hitler
moustache?"

"Yes, exactly. How did you know?"

"Just tell him to give me a break, just this once. It's my thirty-fifth birthday
party, for Chrissake."

"Okay, bud, got it covered."

His trusty cousin, Dylan, was good with people. Brady was confident
that he'd handle Anderson. One thing Brady wasn't going to do was to engage
with that sniveling little toad on his birthday. The minute the police arrived and
slapped the tag on the front door Brady knew who was responsible. This was the
third time in the last six years. "That's it. He's toast." As soon as the cops had left,
he went straight to the safe, got his gun, a Colt 45, walked across the road, rang
the doorbell and, when Anderson's wife opened the door, brushed past her and
entered the living room where Anderson was drinking a glass of brandy. The look
on his face when Brady pointed the gun at him was priceless. Brady would never
forget the way his hairy nose began twitching in squirrel-like fashion. Brady shot
him in the ankle, turned around, and went home. Half an hour later he was in
police custody. As he was being taken handcuffed into the interview room, he
saw two plant pots which belonged in his front yard.

"How are you feeling, William?" Gillian had been married to Anderson for
forty-six years, and he'd always been an anal son of a gun. On their very first date,

he'd left the restaurant six times to check on his car. The only available space in the parking lot was next to a badly parked, beat-up Datsun pick-up, and he was nervous that the guy would scrape him when leaving. He even wrote the plate number down.

He had been operated on, the bullet had to be removed, and a metal plate inserted to hold his shattered ankle in place. The prognosis wasn't bad. He'd need extensive physio and would be able to walk reasonably freely, although possibly with a slight limp. "I'm fine, my treasure. Have those in 2820 done anything about their peeling paint yet?"

"Oh, for God's sake, William. This has just got to stop. Are you really looking to get yourself killed?"

"Of course not, my treasure. I just want folks to face up to their responsibilities. I'm the only one that keeps them honest."

"Honest? Did you say honest? Brady Wilkerson was acting honestly, was he? I tell you now, William, I refuse to carry on living like this. I'm going to go home, destroy all your stupid codes and ordinances, and then call Daisy and tell her you'd like to rejoin the bridge game."

"But my treasure, I can't poss....."

"I'm not interested, William. See you tomorrow." She'd left the hospital ward before he could get another word out.

Brady rolled over onto his back and lit up a cigarette. Cat, reaching for her black polka dot babydoll, said, "Well, all the worry hasn't affected your performance, honey, so that's one good thing at least."

"Spose." Brady was due in court the following day and was deeply anxious. "Hell, what a stupid ass I am. Anderson played me like a fiddle. It was as though he wanted me to do something extreme. I might be an idiot, but that guy's such a loser. Spending his whole life with his nose in other people's business. What motivates a guy like that? I mean, it's like he just wants to be at war with fucking everyone."

"Good question, Bray. I was thinking the same thing. I reckon he's caught up in a loveless marriage and is probably very unhappy with his life. I bet he hasn't had sex in years. Plus, I don't think he actually does anything. Didn't he used to work for the electric company?   "Dunno. What I do know is he needs help.

Even more than I do. Hey, Cat, I know, send him a list of shrinks anonymously. I'd love to see the look on his face." Brady laughed out loud, choking himself as the smoke poured out of his mouth and nose and into his dilated, bloodshot eyes.

John and his pal, Dennis, were enjoying a hot midnight Jacuzzi at the latter's condo at River and Campbell. Dennis had skinned up European style, half tobacco, half the killer green bud or KGB, as he liked to refer to it. "Brady's gotta man up, start showing up for his life. After he's through with these three years he'll have spent five of the last eight years in the can. Now that's not clever. Know what I'm saying," said John.

"Sure, I know what you're saying, man, but the question is: Can a guy like that ever change? I mean, how many chances does he want? One thing I do know. He has to get some anger management classes. Bet he can do that in the clink." Dennis pulled hard on the joint. It tasted real good. Definitely some of the best stuff he'd had in quite a while. Light and spongy and with a great, woody aroma. Must get some of this "purple haze" again, he thought.

"You're right, Dude. He should do some of that therapy shit. I've defended him in the past, and after he shot Anderson I can't say I was sorry because the guy's such a dork. But, really, what Brady did was mad. And you know what, the way he just walked over there and shot him was weird. It's like he wasn't even flipping out. He just did it coldly, you know, not exactly premeditated, but he was in total control. Now that's the kind of thing that scares me.....Hey, Dennis, don't bogart the joint, man."

Coogan was delighted. The crunch aggravation-mitigation hearing had gone entirely according to plan. Gilbert had given coherent evidence about how Anderson had made his life hell over a six-month period. The prosecution had dug up Joe Harper, an old foe of Brady's from high school, who claimed that Brady had been violent towards him on several occasions. He had allegedly tortured him by repeatedly shoving his head into the toilet bowl and, on another occasion, had stabbed him multiple times with a fork, causing a wound that required twenty-eight stitches. Much to the dismay of the prosecution, Harper expressed his delight that Brady would be serving a lengthy prison term. His aggressive vengefulness contrasted sharply with the contrition expressed by Brady at the earlier plea hearing. The other big result for Coogan was that the victim of the assault that resulted in Brady's previous conviction was himself now in prison for a violent offence. That information had been teased out of the prosecution by the judge and rather begged the question as to why they were so anxious to contest Brady's mitigating circumstances claim.

As Brady lay on his cell bed, he reflected for the zillionth time on his stupidity. "You fucking macho piece of shit. So you finally shot somebody. Feel good, does it? You're a loser, Brady, and everyone knows it. It's last chance saloon time. What you gonna do about it? Huh? You gonna sink without a trace or find within you a nugget of self-respect and motivation? He sure as hell had been lucky to find Coogan. Instead of seven years, he'd gotten away with three and a half, and he would more than likely have to serve eighty or eighty-five percent of that. So he was looking at around three years before he could again taste freedom. He'd be thirty by then. He'd have every incentive to make sure he didn't squander the fourth decade of his life, as he'd most certainly done with the third.

At least he wasn't the meat in a bunk bed sandwich this time. And his new cellmate was a middle class guy in for tax evasion. They'd already cut a deal. Brady was going to teach him about fixing shit, anything from toilets to toasters to wiring, and, in return, he would school Brady in how to run a business. If he could make it out of the long, dark tunnel ahead, and he would fight with every sinew of his body to do so, he was quietly confident that he would eventually find a way to flourish beneath his beloved Sonoran sunshine.

The Bolshevik

"I think we mustn't underestimate the degree of political awareness that Lenin believed was required before the conditions were ripe for revolution. He didn't advocate just going to factories and trying to initiate spontaneous action. That's why an educated vanguard was needed. It was essential to feed off the ideas of bourgeois intellectuals like Kant and Hegel."

Trevor Stevenson was in his element as he held forth on his hero, Lenin, to the eight or nine other attendees of the discussion on Marxism at Revolutionary Grounds coffee shop on Fourth Avenue. A mixture of ivory-tower academics, lifelong trade unionists, hardened communist party members, regular blue-collar workers, and younger neophytes listened to him.

Jeff, a white-haired man wearing glasses that looked like swimming goggles, chipped in. "Trevor's right. Lenin was not an economic determinist like Marx. Ideas and politics were all important. Ideologically pure cadres were the drivers of the revolution."

A young guy wearing a red bandana and red cookie-cutter Che t-shirt spoke up. "So, like, with Marx, did he approve of Lenin's actions in 1917?"

Norman, a diminutive man with buck teeth and huge, flappy ears, was quick to respond. "Well, obviously he'd been dead for a long time by then, but it's an interesting question. I reckon he'd have had mixed feelings. On the one hand, his predictions about a country having to be highly industrialized before a revolution could succeed was proved wrong but, on the other hand, I'm sure he'd have been delighted that the Tsarists were overthrown and the revolution succeeded. And he would certainly see confirmation today that his projections about the ever increasing internal contradictions within capitalism were being realized."

Everyone, except the bandana boy, nodded sagely.

"Good to see you smiling again, Trev. I can't remember the last time," said Norman, one of the Marxists.

"Neither can I, Norm. Neither can I."

Stevenson shook his head slowly, smoothing down his wafer thin hair in the process. He was 6' 2," had a light complexion, and was all skin and bone. He walked with a loping gait and at such an acute angle to the ground that it often looked like he was on the verge of toppling over. Stevenson stepped out onto the sidewalk, thoroughly invigorated and as convinced as he'd ever been of the rightness of the Marxist model. The bi-weekly meetings with kindred spirits invariably sent the blood running through his veins. In fact, the high was as good as any high he'd ever had when snorting the good old Colombian marching powder back in the day. He strolled south on Fourth in the direction of his favorite watering hole, The Shanty bar, a laid-back retro venue, full of brass and mirrors, with a decidedly upscale feel to it. It was located directly opposite the once grandiose Mission style Coronado Hotel, which was now a pink but decaying flophouse.

En route, he passed the only other place in town he visited regularly, the Book Stop; a musty, labyrinthine store, brim full of secondhand books on every topic imaginable. Its pièce de résistance was an ornate brass National cash register that was almost a hundred years old and still worked perfectly.

Stevenson was an unreconstructed Bolshevik. Born and raised in the Midwest industrial belt, he belonged to good, solid, working-class stock. The father and grandfather had been firefighters, the mother a nurse, and the grandmother a social worker. *When did the phrase "working class" become a dirty word?* Stevenson was always asking himself. Nowadays, it was all about the middle class. Obama referenced them in almost every speech he made. But try and find any reference to the working class in mainstream American political discourse, and you were struggling. That fact pissed Stevenson off. To hardened class warriors like him, the working class was not some fad or cyclical phenomenon. It was a permanent feature of any society worthy of the name; an indispensable agent of human progress. As long as men donned overalls and sweated blood to extract minerals from beneath the earth's crust, and as long as women sewed and weaved and pummeled, there would be a working class.

February 2011 had gone a long way towards restoring Stevenson's faith in working class dynamism. The mass protests in Madison, Wisconsin, his home town, in response to its Tea Party governor's assault on public sector workers were a breath of fresh air, and the Arab spring was the finest example of the indomitable spirit of the oppressed masses yet seen in the 21st century. Stevenson and many of his comrades were upbeat. Moist-eyed and suddenly recalling the halcyon days of 1960s activism, they were reminded of the old adage about hope springing eternal. But at the same time they were too experienced to allow their warm feelings of nostalgia to blind them to the reality that capital would fight back hard and fight back dirty, just like it always did—just like any behemoth backed into a corner always would. With the exception of 1917 in Russia and 1959 in Cuba, the Left knew all about false dawns. It is no different for long suffering supporters of a team of perennial nearly men who know not to get too carried away when reaching the quarters or semis of a major cup.

It was a few days after the occupation of the Wisconsin Statehouse and Stevenson was still feeling bullish. In the Safeway parking lot at Prince and Campbell he noticed a bumper sticker on a huge Dodge pickup. It read: "SOCIALISM WORKS—UNTIL YOU RUN OUT OF OTHER PEOPLE'S MONEY." His first reaction was to laugh out loud, but his feelings of contempt for the owner of the car soon came to the fore. He just stood there looking at the sticker for five or ten minutes, glancing around to see if the driver was approaching and seeing if he could guess who it might be. Part of him sought confrontation, but his self-preservation instinct told him not to act stupid, that it was bound to be some kind of redneck who would likely be armed. Stevenson walked back to his car, found a piece of paper and a pen and wrote: "CAPITALISM HAS END STAGE CANCER—THE RED TIDE IS RISING." He then strolled back to the Dodge and placed his slogan under one of the windshield wipers. He waited in his car for quite a while but no one came. He chuckled to himself for days and wondered how the recipient had reacted. *Maybe I should've put my number on the paper*, he thought.

Political developments may have offered some temporary relief, but they didn't alter the fact that Stevenson was an unhappy and unfulfilled fifty-eight-year-old man. He felt put upon, as though the whole world was against him. He often found himself looking up to the heavens and saying, "Somebody up there doesn't like me," after which he would immediately reprimand himself.

"Stevenson, you fucking ass, what are you saying? You're a card-carrying atheist. There ain't no one up there."

How he'd craved something new, some magical elixir to revive him, to dislodge the stubborn fog of malaise in which he'd been shrouded for a good three years. The fact that he was ambivalent about Tucson didn't help. He'd arrived in the Old Pueblo full of optimism six years ago to take up a post as a lecturer in political science at the University of Arizona. Things had gone well for the first three years. He was popular with students, who responded to his relaxed demeanor and self-deprecating humor.

"You dipstick, Stevenson, you've only gone and copied the wrong chapter— no Hershey's malt balls for you for at least a week."

This was one of his lecture hall lines, usually delivered as light relief when he was struggling to use a DVD player or an overhead projector. Because, make no mistake about it, Stevenson was a true Luddite and completely useless when it came to using technology. He'd had to tell some rather large untruths to get the job at the U of A. Not least that he could navigate his way around a range of Microsoft applications. The truth was the only electronic devices he owned were a Casio calculator, a Sony Boom Box, and a Wahl beard trimmer.

Stevenson had pretty much always been physically healthy. He'd only ever been in a hospital twice: once as an eight-year-old when he'd had his tonsils out and again in his mid-twenties when he'd had a cartilage operation. He rarely went to the doctor. He felt he was healthy enough.

Mentally, the water was muddier. His thirties had not gone all that well. There had been both financial problems—he'd had a condo foreclosed on and run up huge credit card debt—and a devastating relationship breakdown. His wife of eighteen months left him for another man and this broke his heart. He went into a steep decline, suffering bouts of debilitating depression and twice checked himself into a psych ward when dark ideas of suicide entered his head.

He emerged from the slough of despond but there were scars. He was heavily reliant on anti-depressants and therapy but still suffered from some very dark periods during which he'd lie on his bed for days, surrounded by silence, stuffing himself with chips and popcorn. He was in the grip of a sadistic demon that occupied his head and taunted him mercilessly.

Why did you let her go? How can you not have seen it coming? I'll tell you why; because you are so damned self-obsessed. It was all about your intellect, your wit, your writings. You didn't see your wife's jewelry designs. Or her cake recipes. You had it coming, you prick. And you chronically mismanaged your condo situation. You had a chance to re-finance and you blew it. What a loser.

For at least a dozen years after the marriage ended, Stevenson had struggled to hold down a job. The highpoint was an eighteen month sojourn at the University of Kentucky, but he was eventually dismissed for failing to produce the requisite amount of academic papers. He subsequently worked in a Geico call center, sold Hilton Hotel gold cards, and cleaned carpets. The U of A job was the first academic job Stevenson had applied for in nine years. His brother, who worked in educational administration, had cajoled him into going for it. Stevenson never expected a reply. When they short-listed him and then called him for an interview he was astounded. At the interview, he decided that honesty was the best policy and didn't conceal the fact that he'd been despondent for quite a while due to an unfortunate sequence of events. When they offered him the job he seriously wondered if the whole thing wasn't a cruel plot by some academic he may have inadvertently slighted and that when he arrived for his first day's work he would be humiliated and told that it had all been a huge mistake.

Later on, he learned that the department head had been very impressed with the lecture series on Marx he'd written at Kentucky. Apparently, there'd been some opposition to his appointment, but the boss had his way. Worth having a safe, if unspectacular, pair of hands to complement the bright young things had been his argument.

For the first time in ages Stevenson dared to believe that he had a decent shot at turning his life around. One thing was for sure, he was fed up with being in the doldrums. He'd always felt that he was one of life's underachievers. True, his roots were humble, but he'd never reached the heights suggested by his early promise.

The stroke had very nearly done him in. It was a left hemispherical ischemic stroke caused by undetected high blood pressure. He was unconscious for five days, and, at one point, the doctors had been pessimistic. But he miraculously pulled through, and, due to the fact that the right side of the brain controls the ability to exercise judgment, logic, and rationality, those vital faculties were unaffected. However, he was left with intermittent slurring of speech, numbness on the right side of his face, and hand-eye coordination problems. The stroke slowed him down. Everything he did took twice as long. He could walk, but shakily, and he needed a walking stick. Driving a car was out of the question.

Stevenson had to downgrade from his stylish adobe apartment in Armory Park to a fairly shabby studio out east at Alvernon and 29th. But at least he could rely on a monthly social security payment so the slide into destitution was avoided. The department had been sympathetic, and his colleagues chipped in to buy him a limited edition, leather-bound copy of *Das Capital*, which cheered him up. But the sad reality was that Stevenson was a broken man. He had physiotherapy once a week and saw his shrink regularly, which at least got him out of the house. What he was enduring now was even worse than his previous foray into the dark side. At least then he'd been young enough to harbor hopes of rebuilding his life, however deeply embedded they might have been, when he was at his lowest ebb.

Stevenson just could not come to terms with what had happened to him. How could he never have given his health a minute's thought? What did he think he was? Immortal? Christ, he'd been within an inch of dying. Maybe it would've been better if he had. Because, now, what was there ahead of him? He was pretty much useless. Couldn't work, couldn't drive, and was reliant on welfare to keep him afloat, and a lack of funds would condemn him to a largely sedentary and solitary life.

Since his divorce he'd never even come close to a relationship of substance. But there had at least been the odd, short-lived dalliance. Now, he was singularly unappealing. What woman in her right mind would give him the time of day?

He wasn't suicidal although he wasn't exactly sure why. The shrink said it was because he'd come so close to an involuntary death that he couldn't morally entertain the idea of taking his own life. To do so would be to fly in the face of fate or the gods or some higher power that had decreed it wasn't yet his time. Stevenson, of course, wasn't buying into that kind of superstition.

He cried a lot, something he'd never done before. The huge element of self-pity, a new emotion for him, was the catalyst for his lachrymosity. He would find himself sniffling in the supermarket line or on the bus, and there didn't seem to be a damn thing he could do about it. He inhabited a world of grey, grinding, miserableness. He no longer smiled or laughed, even at his own quirkiness. He used to read avidly, watch documentaries, and engage with the pressing issues of the day. But now he'd flick through glossy magazines, watch vapid daytime TV, and generally shuffle around the apartment cleaning and tidying.

In the summer, Stevenson sat in his back yard cross-legged in the scruffy backyard and hose himself down. He'd never gotten used to the heat in Tucson. It was as though the life force was sucked out of him, and all that was left was an inert mass of boiling flesh. The small, square-shaped yard was demarcated by cinderblocks to the west, rusty cyclone fencing to the north, and an incongruous concave wooden fence to the east. A panoply of dense, invasive weeds and wildflowers were threatening to run riot, *Day of the Triffids*-style: yellow star thistle, hairy lotus, Mexican strangletop, little mallow, and purslane, which he regularly mixed with coriander and natural yogurt and ate as a salad. He'd acquired the taste as a child after his father suggested it had healing properties and, sure enough, his acne had disappeared. The solitary jewel amidst these plebeian offerings was a true aristocrat; an elegant, pyramid-like *Agave gracilipes*, teeth running menacingly along the edges of its large leaves.

Stevenson plodded on with life in pedestrian fashion, deprived of the innate quality that had made him the man he once was. As time wore on he began to show signs of rediscovering his former self. He'd meet Paul, one of his old students, once a month and they would play backgammon and talk about politics. Obama mania was taking hold and nearly everyone on the liberal left was excited. It was Paul who told him about Revolutionary Grounds bookshop and invited him to a meeting. Occasionally, he'd go to the movies or a book reading, and he liked to feed the pigeons in his local park. He still used a walking stick but was moving much more freely.

One day he was waiting for the bus when he noticed that the young girl sitting next to him in the shelter was reading Rousseau's *The Social Contract*. His heart missed a beat.

"Err...err. Excuse me. I couldn't help noticing that you're reading Rousseau. I used to teach politics at the U of A. Are you studying it?" He felt like an idiot and was expecting to be given short shrift.

"Oh, wow, that's cool. Yeah, I'm doing a liberal arts degree at Pima Community College. Politics is one of my electives." She smiled an innocent, slightly lopsided smile. She had large, hazel colored eyes, and her brown hair was worn up and held together by a fetching electric-blue scrunchie.

"Do you like it?" Stevenson asked.

"Yeah, I love it, actually. It's really varied. We've already covered Plato, Hobbes, the French Revolution, and totalitarianism."

"That all sounds great. What about Marx and Lenin?"

"Umm, well, I don't think we're doing that in 101. It's probably next semester. That's communism, right?"

"Exactly. I think you'll find it interesting, and it's especially relevant now, what with capitalism being in crisis."

"Oh, is that right? I didn't know about that. I mean, I heard about property prices crashing, and there are so many people who are losing their homes."

"You're right on the money. That's all part of it."

They rode the bus together and the conversation flowed so easily that Stevenson was emboldened to offer her the chance to talk about communism and socialism ahead of the second semester. She said she'd like to do that.

Their relationship was purely platonic. From Carrie's point of view it was a rare opportunity to interact with an older person who had so much time and knowledge to share with her. She was the very first person in her family to study for a degree, and she was determined to make a success of it. Stevenson was a rather serious person, as well as being cultured and polite to people. He was certainly the only person she knew who called bus drivers "sir" or "madam." And it was great that sex had nothing to do with it. She was sick and tired of guys hitting on her, even when they already knew she was in a relationship.

Meeting Carrie energized Stevenson. Her enthusiasm and relaxed demeanor rubbed off on him. She came without baggage, and they appeared to have formed an entirely equitable friendship. And he remembered all over again how deeply satisfying it was to impart knowledge to a receptive young student.

Stevenson delighted in taking his new companion to the Shanty. They played foosball and pool and sipped schnapps on the leafy patio. Stevenson felt lightheaded and became nostalgic as he recalled his carefree undergraduate days in Pittsburgh. They went to the Tanque Verde Swap Meet, a huge outdoor flea market on a thirty acre site, and had a ball. They walked through the throngs and Stevenson could hardly believe his eyes at the vast array of often bizarre items offered. Among the things that caught his eye were a stuffed moose head, geometric instruments, motocross boots, a moving wire lamb with Christmas lights on top of a Maytag washing machine, and a Betty Boop clutch bag. He went home with a Shakespeare baseball cap and a battery operated miniature model of Ray Charles singing and playing the piano.

"This is incredible. Never seen anything like it in my life," said Stevenson. He and Carrie were taking part in the *El Dia de los Muertos* parade, along with thousands of their fellow Tucsonans.

"I told you it was sick. Ha ha! Look at you, you really are like a kid running wild in a candy store."

"Sick? What's sick, Carrie?" Stevenson frowned.

"Sick means awesome in this sense, Trevor."

"Oh, right. I dunno. You youngsters are increasingly unfathomable to me."

He was spellbound by the massive skulls on stilts, painted faces, pirate masks, and cartoon characters.

"This whole thing makes you confront your mortality head on, doesn't it?" he said.

"Exactly. And the idea of celebrating the lives of those who've passed on instead of being miserable and mourning for ages is just perfect."

"Umm...fascinating. I guess if you embrace death rather than fear it, you're releasing yourself from that huge taboo that people are petrified of facing up to."

"Right on, Trevor. I knew bringing you hear would be a good move. So, tell me, do you fear death?"

"Well, that's a good question. At times, yes, but more from a general fear of the unknown as opposed to a faith-based fear of being punished in an afterlife. I came very close to death and, for quite a while, I was so low I wished I'd died. But now I'm quite relaxed about life and death issues. When it's my time to go, I think I'll be ready. What about you, Carrie?"

"I've always thought about the moment of dying, when you take your last breath, and that scares me. As for what comes next, I think it depends how you look at it. If you consider death as a kind of moving on to a higher level of consciousness it doesn't seem so scary. But I can't deny that sometimes I worry about dying."

"Interesting. We should talk more about it. This whole Day of the Dead thing has been a real revelation for me. I might even dress up for it next year." As he was speaking, his eyes were following a guy in a yellow pinstriped suit and skeleton mask who was carrying a violin case; and then, a ghoulish looking man who'd painted half of his face white and half black and divided the two with a huge streak of red.

Although Carrie had shown him a side of Tucson he didn't know existed, he still needed more convincing.

"What's so great about Tucson, Carrie? I just don't get it. Okay, there's the U of A campus, Fourth Avenue, and the swap meet, but as far as I can see the rest is just miles and miles of nondescript roads running in straight lines chock full of gas stations, 7-11s, K-Marts, hair and nail salons, tattoo parlors, pawn shops, payday loan sharks, and fast food outlets."

She laughed. "Trevor, there's so much here, you'd be amazed. Where to start? Mount Lemmon, the Desert Museum, the Botanical Gardens, Old Tucson Film Studios, Tucson Museum of Art, the Gem Show, KXCI Community Radio. I could go on, but hopefully you get the point."

"Guess I may have underestimated this place. Sorry, Tucson," said Stevenson earnestly.

"The thing is you're not alone. A lot of folks make the same mistake of writing Tucson off too quickly. You just have to explore, and you'll find plenty of good stuff. The way I usually describe it is that Tucson is so much more than the sum of its parts."

"Oh, I like that, Carrie, very nicely put." *Carrie and Tucson are both surprise packages*, he thought.

She went back to school with the edge over her fellow students, her head full of false consciousness and dialectical materialism. He missed not seeing her, but they were firm friends, and he expected them to remain so.

The red diaper babies, as the offspring of Marxists were once called, were very excited by the advent of the Occupy Wall Street movement. Turned out Wisconsin was only an appetizer. Occupy Wall Street was the real deal; a chink in the capitalist armor. Finally, a real chance to build a broad coalition capable of challenging the corporate hegemony.

Stevenson was downtown at the movement's Veinte de Agosto Park encampment. Looking around, he saw a big, colorful Occupy Tucson banner, dozens of anti-Wall Street signs, a sprinkling of tents, water tanks, piles of political literature, dogs wearing knitted Occupy Wall Street jackets, meditation, solar cooking, and a healthy turnout—maybe a hundred folks. *This movement rocks*, he thought. He loved the way everything the organizer said was repeated back to her by the whole crowd, apparently a tactic used by Occupy Wall Street where loudspeakers aren't available.

The event was the start of a nationwide "move your money" campaign in which people were encouraged to move their money from the major banks to small banks and credit unions. The group marched through the financial district, chanting slogans. Stevenson was in full voice, as he sang; "Banks got bailed out, we got sold out," and "The people united will never be divided." Outside JP Morgan Chase, Wells Fargo, and Bank of America mock citations were issued to the banks for crimes against the American people. A posh British gentleman in a pinstriped suit played the role of the slimy, sinister banker.

Stevenson had long reflected on the fact that he would leave no legacy in this world. No offspring, no original ideas, no books, only a handful of short pieces in political periodicals. Was it too late to salvage the situation? Did he have any creative impulse left within him, or was he just a burnt-out relic whose only claims to fame were an honors degree from the University of Pittsburgh and a salesman of the month award for selling those goddamn Hilton Hotel gold cards? He remembered the manager's spiel even now:

"Right, folks. Big push for the power hour. Let's go!"

I wonder what became of him, thought Stevenson. *He's probably one of the elite one percent who is responsible for the impending Armageddon. Or maybe he was one of those who were screwed by his own kind, by Madoff; now that would be funny.*

But maybe now none of that mattered. If he could be part of something so huge that it could really break the capitalist mold and fashion a new, infinitely more egalitarian state of affairs, then that would satisfy him. He could exit stage left a contented man. A new political settlement beckoned. Stevenson was sure of it. Of course, the State and its apparatchiks would unleash the usual tools of oppression, and blood would be spilled—it always was—but make no mistake, this time they had a real fight on their hands. This movement would not fade away, its day in the sun merely a warm memory. At long last he had a raison d'être, something tangible to latch on to. He felt alive and in the world. He had emerged, he could now safely say, from a long hibernation.

By the end of 2011 the forces for change were in retreat. On home soil, the Occupy movement had been clubbed and pepper sprayed out of its parallel parkland universe. In the Middle East, the Arab Spring's initial surge had been repulsed by the forces of darkness, which had no compunction about dragging half-naked women along the street and forcibly extracting the fingernails and toenails of brave revolutionaries. Stevenson, so clear-sighted and sanguine in the autumn, was now deeply depressed. He'd been diagnosed with valley fever and would spend days on end in a drugged-up, semi-conscious, haze. In his rare lucid moments, his heart would sink every time he read the news.

And then Stevenson's father visited him—for the very first time since he passed on nine years earlier.

"Well boy, this is your moment. Make sure you don't waste it now," he was saying.

"Dad, you know me. I could no more stand idly by and let this seminal moment pass than could you." His father was smiling broadly.

"Atta boy. I knew I could count on you to keep the family tradition going." But then, he became serious. "But you haven't got kids. It's all going to die out. Come on son, it's not too late. There are lots of older fathers these days."

"But Dad, it's too late for me now. We must find other ways of keeping our legacy going. Don't be too hard on me Dad."

It was more than a dream, he was sure of it. His father was there, right in front of him, in high-definition. He was wearing his firefighters' uniform, and he was clean-shaven. Stevenson had tried to reach out and stroke him, but he'd been powerfully restrained. He was in a straitjacket, being squeezed. He felt so very tight. In the background was a huge demonstration, and he could see the Wisconsin State Capitol. There were miners with their blackened faces, strapping firefighters, and nurses in their scrubs. There were banners everywhere and the noise was deafening. And then he woke up.

He was shaking like a leaf, worn out. Now, more than ever, he had to be resolute. He wanted to show his father that he meant business. He resolved that as soon as he felt strong enough, he would head for Madison for the first time in twenty years. *Back to the rust belt it is, then,* he said to himself. *This old class-warrior will live to fight another day.*

Love Letters From A Bandit

At the station—smoke
The red lights of the train
The breath of the three
Guards hanging on the blue air
Your unshaven chin
Roughing my ear
As I listen to the click of your accents
Your lips warm with words
Yet to be spoken
Before the journey, its separation

You have jumped clear
A waving figure receding.
The train whistle rising into the mist
Like a dead prayer
Played with by so many enduring minarets
The great domed mosques
Leaning into heaviness
The rolling waters of the harbor
Turkish violin music

Snow erupts in the faces of buildings
The rhythms
Of these iron wheels
The helplessness in your black eyes
Pulling me steadily into the wilderness
I watch your features
Form and dissolve
In the milky changes of the glass
Proud Kurdish features
Forever to be memorized.
      —Sheri Laizer, "1986, Sirkeci Train Station, Istanbul" in
Martyrs, Traitors and Patriots (1991) Jaf Press, London.

1995

Ever since her loved one, Erdal, had been incarcerated in Merter Prison in Istanbul, Clare was all at sea. Her soul ached, and although she was physically back in the Occident, spiritually she was far away, in the Orient. She would often sit with her eyes closed, conjuring up images and lamentations born in the Levant. Istanbul was the city of her dreams, a colossus straddling Europe and Asia, its indelible footprint permeating the annals of world history. In the year she'd lived there Clare would often drink Turkish coffee at Ortaköy. She loved to sit in the shadow of the immense Bosphorus Bridge, a suspension bridge that spanned the onyx blue Strait along which, myth has it, Ulysses passed. And yet, nagging away at her was the dark underbelly of a place in which there were as many gaunt political prisoners trudging, heads bowed, around desolate Anatolian prison courtyards as there were minarets and shoe-shine boys.

"I'm sorry darling, I really can't help you and, to be honest, I don't understand how someone in your position can afford to be so generous. I know you care about people but these one woman crusades of yours are getting beyond a joke."

"Mom, I love this man. I've never loved anyone in this way before. I want to spend the rest of my life with him. And what the hell do you mean by 'one woman crusades?' The last time I helped anybody was two years ago when I leant Omar two hundred fifty bucks to pay for his tuition fees. That hardly makes me a saint."

"Kiddo, you don't know what you're saying. You meet a penniless, trigger-happy Turkish gangster type and he's the one you decide to throw your lot in with. What possible future can there be in it? Makes no sense to me."

"He made a mistake and he's paying the price for it now, big time. I promise you, he's a good person and he's ambitious. He's just had a rough time and got corrupted by the wrong people. Everyone deserves a second chance, don't they? Come on Mom, open your heart. I swear to God I'll work hard and pay you back. Every penny."

"Honey, I've given you my reasons. I'm not going to change my mind. And even if I wanted to help I can't spare that kind of dough right now. I've got to find four grand for the yard paving."

"The guy's behind bars, for God's sake and he's got nobody. His family disowned him and it's pretty rough in there according to the lawyer, God knows what will happ..."

Clare's voice tailed off as she realized the futility of the whole exercise. When she got home she wept uncontrollably. She'd always been emotional but she'd shed so many tears in recent weeks that she half expected her reserves of salt water to run dry. She really tried hard to see things from her mother's point of view, but the feeling of resentment persisted. It wasn't all that long ago that she really looked up to her. But her mother seemed to have become a mean-spirited person.

Ten months after Clare arrived in Turkey to teach English, Erdal was detained. Apparently, it was in relation to a crime he'd committed seven years earlier. Clare was devastated, and his lawyer had advised her to go back home as there was no bail in Turkey; it existed on paper but was only ever granted to celebrity types. People accused of crimes could languish behind bars for years before they had their day in court. If she was able to contribute some funds, the lawyer would do his utmost to speed things up. But there were no guarantees. Moreover, Erdal had not wanted her to visit him in prison. He said it would have been too painful.

Now, she was back home in her native Tucson, a city of over 700,000 residents in Arizona's Sonoran Desert. Tucson was famously referred to by the Beatles in their song "Get Back." Clare had always been thrilled at the number of people she met overseas who'd heard of Tucson, even if many of them couldn't put their finger on why. Clare never passed up an opportunity to tell them it was likely they knew Tucson because of "Get Back." She would then go on and say that Paul McCartney wrote it and his wife, Linda, studied in Tucson at the University of Arizona. The final piece of information she shared was that, much later, they bought a ranch in Tucson, which Paul still owned.

Erdal was a pretty boy who was blessed with smooth, olive skin, wavy light brown hair, and a dimpled chin. However, his refined looks belied his background as a streetwise Kurdish boy from Diyarbakır, a large, majority Kurdish city in the southeast of Turkey. A neat scar over the left eyebrow and a deeper, serrated one, on the chin were legacies of a violent childhood.   Like many of his friends and family, Erdal became politicized at a very young age. He was beaten up by teachers for speaking Kurdish and jumped by the ultra-nationalist students known as the Grey Wolves. He would be hauled into the cells with hundreds of others for celebrating *Newroz*, the Kurdish New Year, and arrested and beaten for carrying Kurdish newspapers or listening to Kurdish music cassettes. For a while he was involved with both Kurdish political parties and illegal, left-wing revolutionary groups but soon become disillusioned.

Many of his comrades had taken up arms, notably for the Kurdistan Workers Party, known as the PKK. Some of his pals fled abroad, mainly to England or Germany, and others were rotting in prison. Many were killed or "disappeared." Erdal had seen injustice at close quarters and knew what it was to suffer. But he was just not a political animal. He was determined to take an alternative path and had his own long-term strategy; to make it as a businessman. Once he'd established himself he would use his influence to promote the Kurdish cause. Erdal had cut his teeth in his early teens, wheeling and dealing in anything he could get his hands on—cigarettes, leather jackets, saucepans. Now, in his mid-twenties, he was importing Georgian cosmetics.

For seven years Erdal had lived with the guilt of his cowardly shooting of an unarmed man. He'd become involved with some gangster types and they'd pressured him into doing their dirty work. It was the one and only time he'd ever used a weapon and he'd never stopped regretting it. He'd fallen out badly with his ex-fiancée and she'd betrayed him to the police. Behind his back, she'd retrieved the gun from where he'd buried it and kept it until the moment was right to report him. He'd underestimated her malevolence, and now he was going to pay for it. *You live by the sword and you die by it.* Erdal was sick of hearing himself repeat the same old mantra, but now he was going to find out if he could take his punishment like a man. The unexpected thing was that prison would be every bit as enlightening for Erdal as it was brutal. For the first time in his life he read books and learned a skill; carpentry. He began to understand that time is a precious commodity. Contemplation was a whole new experience. Just to sit still with his eyes closed and allow his mind to wander was therapeutic.

Erdal's relationship with Clare spurred him on to improve as a human being and to make sure he never again allowed himself to sink so low. He'd laid eyes on her for the first time as they boarded one of Istanbul's motley army of sea vessels. Hundreds of boats jostled and flirted impossibly with each other as they chugged across the Bosphorus. Erdal had been struck by her porcelain complexion, big green eyes and thick, curly hair. As they waited on the quayside on a bitterly cold November morning, his yellow waterproof jacket stood out against the slate grey sky. He was shivering and smoking frantically, barely inhaling. Clare could not help smiling as she observed the staccato movements of this frail, elf-like figure. Erdal seized the moment by offering her a cigarette.

"Would you like?"

"Okay, thanks."

The two were soon feeling their way gently into a clipped, smoke-ridden conversation. Long pauses are not perceived as such when cigarettes are caressed, tugged at and clinically extinguished.

"Tourist," asked Erdal?

"No, working. I teach English. Just arrived. Five day ago."

"Where it is?"

"Near Taksim Square."

"I know. Good. Where from you?"

"I'm American."

"I know. Good. New York?"

"No, I'm from a city called Tucson. We're in the desert, near Mexico. Do you know what a cactus is? We have many of them." Erdal looked at her blankly. She quickly thumbed through her Turkish-English dictionary, and showed him the entry for desert.

"Yes, yes," he said excitedly. "Çöl, I know çöl. I see in Mısır when I am boy." "Mısır?" Clare inquired.

"Yes, yes. Where is big pyramit. You know, big pyramit."

"Oh, you mean Egypt?"

"Yes, yes. Egypt. Egypt. We say Mısır. Sorry, sorry."

"It's fine."

Clare laughed. Then she showed him the entry for cactus which turned out to be the same word except it was spelled with k's instead of c's.

"Kaktüs. Yes, yes, I know. We have in here. In Turkey. I like too much."

From that day until Erdal was swallowed up by the Turkish state the pair had been inseparable. Intoxicated by love these two youngsters explored Istanbul. They allowed this city of the imagination to immerse them in its kaleidoscope of sights, sounds, and smells. The raucous, incessant, night time conversations of groups of dogs; the crowing of the dawn rooster, followed shortly thereafter by the call to prayer, hovering lugubriously on the wind; the glockenspiel jingle of bottled gas sellers; the oddly endearing sight of vegetable sellers on their trucks, offering their wares through a loudspeaker; gridlocked roads where cars, lorries, yellow New York style taxis, massive old Buicks and Cadillacs—converted into *dolmuş* (shared taxi)—and overloaded, lopsided minibuses fought tooth and nail for space; mirrored tower blocks and shopping malls sprouting up alongside mosques, markets, *hamamlar* (Turkish baths), tea houses, run down car repair garages, tailors, cobblers, and barbers; the unceasing sales patter, barter, and exchange of goods—everything from stethoscopes to live crabs to skis on offer; and the smell of freshly grilled fish, kebabs, herbs and spices, thick, Gauloises-style tobacco smoke, burning coal, petrol fumes, and lemon scented cologne. In Istanbul, the senses were relentlessly and gloriously assaulted.

Six thousand miles away, Clare's home soil comforted her. She loved Tucson's beguiling desert landscape, especially its majestic Saguaro cactus. These towering kings have a life span of up to two hundred years, grow to an average height of thirty feet, and weigh several tons. Ubiquitous and ever present from generation to generation, they serve as reassuring companions to humankind, one of very few constants in a changing world. Clare liked to refer to them as the hedgehogs of the desert because of the sharp spikes that ran along their thick, ribbed stems. Their skin is green and waxy and their multiple arms curve gently skyward, as though in open invitation to the wrens, woodpeckers, and owls that make their homes in their cavernous, water-storing interiors. As if that was not enough, they produce flowers and succulent fruits. Clare would regularly go to the Saguaro National Monument at the foot of the Rincon Mountains at sunset. She loved being surrounded by silhouetted saguaros, as azure blue gave way to a reddish-orange glow, which, in turn, was usurped by the cosmic stillness of the star-filled night sky.

As Clare rediscovered Tucson Erdal was brought before the public prosecutor and pleaded guilty to charges of malicious wounding with a firearm. The good news was that his lawyer, Haluk, was informed that the case was to be heard by a judge in the First Instance Penal Court as opposed to the Heavy Penal Court. This meant that he could only be subject to a maximum two year sentence. However, even if Erdal made it into court quickly there was always the possibility that the judge might come up with an excuse not to hear the case. The wrong stamp on a document, more time needed to evaluate submissions made months earlier by the defense lawyer, and a long delay in the provision of a forensic report were common reasons.

Merter Prison, Istanbul—September 20th 1995

Hayatım (my life) my eyes closed. I not in here, I float on clouds, I see snow on top mountain. Birds under me I can see. I am still in world. I see you, you smile, green eyes, white skin, I feel peaceful when I think you. I have bit of hope. I have one friend, name Ali. He look me, has been inside here many time, his English bit okay, can help me write you. There is one dictionary. Is lucky, no? *Seni seviyorum. Sonsuza kadar* (I love you forever).

Tucson, Arizona—November 17th 1995

Canım benim (my darling). Your letter moved me so much. I know you will forgive me when I say I doubted you. Your strength, your imagination. I know they will never break your spirit. Once this ordeal is over you will never look back. *Dert etme bebeğim. Yakında beraber olacağız* (Don't worry babe. Soon we'll be together). I'm reading Nazim Hikmet. He's wonderful. I forgot to ask you if you've read any of his poems. I really like this one, called "The Bees." What do you think?

> The bees, like big drops of honey carrying grapevines to the
> sun came flying out of my youth; the apples, these heavy
> apples, are also from my youth; the gold-dust road, these
> white pebbles in the stream, my faith in songs, my freedom
> from envy, the cloudless day, this blue day, the sea flat on its
> back, naked and warm, my longing, these bright teeth and full
> lips—they all came to this Caucasian village like big drops of
> honey on the legs of bees out of my youth, the youth I left
> somewhere
> before I was through.

Öpüyorum seni (I kiss you). Clare

Merter Prison, Istanbul—January 5th 1996

Tatlım (my sweet). I am good. All the days I am better. My mind get bigger. I think more. I must to be more slow, in my mind and action. Not to judging so fast. Not to angry. You told me like this. You are clever. I hear my uncle he die heart attack, 47 years. Very terrible. Too many in our country finish life like it. Very big stress because. Everything can happen in here. Earthquake, big politic problem, too many economy *kriz* (crisis). We must to continue. True? Now I go woodwork shop. I build you one ship. Ok? Write me soon. Your *eşkiya* (bandit). I hug with you.

Tucson, Arizona—February 3rd 1996

Balım (my honey). It was great to get your letter. Very sorry to hear about your uncle. Work is good. My beginner class is excellent. I've got students from Mexico, Peru, South Korea, Somalia, and Morocco. The funniest one is a very quiet boy from South Korea. Whenever I ask him a question he spends five minutes looking through his dictionary and then says: "I write answer for you later." My Turkish class is going well. There are eight of us including a diplomat and a girl who works for the Red Cross. We all went to the teacher's house for a Turkish meal the other night. His wife cooked my favorite ıspanaklı börek (spinach pancakes). *Lezzetli oldu* (They were delicious). I should soon be able to send some funds to your lawyer. He told me there is some money in the pot, but every little bit helps, right? Stay strong, *güzelim* (my beautiful).

Merter Prison, Istanbul—June 14th 1996

Gülüm (my rose). Sorry I take long time for write you. I am down before. They bad behave me. I feel peace. I think they no like it. They put light night time and put shit in my book. But I will not tell something. I dream you and me. Keep me strong. Ali is good. Tell good story every day. I laugh to much. *Vay, vay, vay* (wow). You eat ıspanaklı *börek*. I jealous. In here food bad. Same and same *çorba* (soup). Now I am okay. Don't worry me. Bye *meleğim* (my angel).

Tucson, Arizona—September 10th 1996

Herşeyim (my everything). Thank you for your letter. I am glad you are feeling better. I know you are strong. No matter what anyone does to you, you will survive.

I'm fine. Been swimming a lot lately so I'm feeling pretty fit and healthy. Do they let you have much exercise? I'm reading an amazing book at the moment. It's called *A Man* by Oriana Fallaci, an Italian writer. It's about a stormy love affair between herself and Alexander Panagoulis, a Greek poet and political dissident at the time of the military regime. He was imprisoned for trying to assassinate the top general. He was incredible, had a will of iron. They could never break him. I'll try and find out if it's been translated into Turkish.

It was my Mom's birthday last night. We all went out to a Chinese restaurant. I had a bit too much to drink and spilled my wine on Mom's new dress. *Çok sakarım, bunu biliyorsun* (I'm very clumsy. You know this). Never mind, she'll get over it...might take a while though. We haven't been getting along that well recently. *Kendine iyi bak, hayatım* (Take care, my life). Clare

"Yes lady. We wait you, our restaurant ship-shape Bristol fashion, very fresh fish from Bosphorus. Come to the inside and we will make it very special night for you."

Clare loved this guy's sales spiel. Grinning from ear to ear, his white teeth contrasted with his somber black lounge suit and flamboyant tartan waistcoat. But the coup de grace was his moustache. Even bushier than the Turkish standard, it had been groomed to coil up at each end. *A classic nineteenth century Prussian nobleman's moustache*, thought Dot, Clare's best friend and confidante. The waiter had won them over, and as they sat down at the table they already had a good feeling about Kumkapı, an old Ottoman fishing district on the banks of the Marmara Sea that was now famous for its fish restaurants.

The atmosphere was electric. Pedestrians made their way through bustling, narrow walkways between rows and rows of symmetrically arranged tables. The long purple tablecloths, topped off with smaller white paper cloths, looked from a distance like an army of hooded priests. Boisterous diners—many downing the milky white, 50 proof, aniseed flavored Rakı—clapped and sang along as they were serenaded by itinerant troubadours and musicians.

"You have comfort ladies? Don't worry. By and by we bring you too much food and drink. But now you try our famous lion milk, yes? It makes you strong and bold."

The girls were already giggling at the waiter's colonial style English. "He's probably got some ancient text book, maybe I'll get to know him better and then I'll find out." Dot winked mischievously.

"You're such a dark horse, Dotty. I thought you said all that getting down and dirty with Turkish waiters and Italian tour guides was behind you."

Clare pushed and pulled the older girl affectionately. They'd met nine years ago at a salsa class in San Francisco. Dot was from blue-chip Connecticut stock and her father was a judge, whereas Clare was the offspring of a car salesman and a pastry chef. Despite the twelve year age gap and different upbringings they'd hit it off instantly. Clare liked Dot's dry, self-deprecating humor, while Dot was taken by Clare's say-what-you mean directness. Dot had given up an all-expenses-paid week in Tunisia with a wealthy Middle Eastern suitor so that she could be with Clare at Erdal's court hearing in Istanbul.

As the girls strolled back to the hotel they noticed how affectionate Turkish people were with each other. They saw two young male friends walking along, one with his arm resting on the other's shoulders and they saw a young woman in a traditional Islamic headscarf walking arm in arm with another woman wearing trendy western clothing, makeup, and jewelry. They were agreed that it was heartening to see and spoke volumes for the unique nature of Turkish society.

They turned a corner and came across a gaggle of around twenty-five people standing next to a coach. Most of them were middle-aged women who were weeping and wailing. One of them was kneeling on the sidewalk, praying. Every now and then she would raise herself up and slap her forehead with the palms of her hands. Another hauntingly hollow-eyed woman in a headscarf simply stretched her arms out towards the coach in quiet desperation. Others waved or mouthed goodbyes to their loved ones on the coach. All of the passengers were crop-haired young men. Most of them, seemingly impervious to the commotion outside, continued reading their newspapers or just looked diffidently into space.

"Ne oluyor?" (What's happening) Clare asked another bystander.

"Asker, asker," (soldier) was the reply.

"Of course. They're going off to do their military service. That's tough," said Clare.

She had no idea whether Erdal had done his military service. There was still so much about him she didn't know.

It had taken fifteen months for Erdal to finally get into court for sentencing. Haluk was confident that the chances of immediate release were good, although there was always the possibility that a hard-line judge would make him serve the maximum twenty-four months. Courtroom 36 was cold and bare. There was a witness stand which reminded Clare of the pulpit in her local church. The walls were whitewashed and windowless. There was a single strip light, stripy grey and black linoleum flooring, and the obligatory picture of the ubiquitous Mustafa Kemal Ataturk, founder of the Turkish Republic, in a heroic pose. On a lopsided shelf sat a bottle of the popular lemon cologne. The pièce de résistance, however, as out of place as a zebra caught up in a herd of wildebeest, was an exquisite mahogany desk, replete with gold-plated latticework.

His bones may have been damp but Erdal's heart leapt when he saw Clare in court. All of a sudden his two escorts, one of whom he was handcuffed to, were no longer there. How quickly lightness can eclipse heaviness and claustrophobia and turn into boundlessness.

"What's going on Dot? Why is the judge waving his finger like that and shaking his head?" Clare was deathly pale and beginning to hyperventilate. Dot put her arm around her friend and snuggled up to her.

"Come on honey. Try to hold it together. You've got to, for Erdal's sake." As she was speaking, she looked down at her low cut, pink and white chiffon number and immediately regretted her inappropriate attire. The hearing lasted no more than five minutes, and before they knew it, Erdal had been led out of court, and the judge had retreated. Haluk looked gloomy.

"What happened?" asked Clare.

"Not good today, Clare *Hanım* (Miss Clare). Judge was too hard. Decided case will be transferred to Heavy Penal Court. Soon, we have new hearing."

"What does that mean?" Clare felt her chest tighten.

"Unfortunately, in other court he might be face longer sentence."

"Oh Christ. How long, Haluk?"

"Might be three years."

"Oh hell. What can we do? There must be something we can do." Tears ran down Clare's face and her dark teal eyeliner began to smudge.

"Well, I think we have chance to do something. I had arranged everything with first judge. But he no come today. Don't know why. I will contact to him again."

"I beg you, Haluk. I beg you. Get him out soon." Clare's voice cracked and she wept into her chest.

Şişli, Istanbul—January 4th 1997

Bir tanem (my number one). I believe in you. I know you're going through hell but I know you'll come out of it a stronger person. You'll be able to turn everything you've experienced in prison to your advantage. Close your eyes and imagine we are walking along the beach, the vast expanse of ocean in front of us. Together, we can reach our promised land. I am staying here in Istanbul. My school is giving me plenty of teaching hours. Keep the faith. Clare.

Yavrucum (my little one). I scar. I know, did big mistake. But I take big punish, when is end? I believe Haluk. He good man. Maybe he help me still. I prey. Ali is good. He make joke every time. One day he say, he show us his place, in *Gelibolu* (Gallipoli). You know, where we won in war. I touch you. Smell you. I feel good.

Three months later, Clare and Dot had put another fifteen hundred dollars into the kitty. Haluk had pulled some strings and managed to have the case reinstated in the First Instance Penal Court. He was hopeful they could get back into court within eight or nine weeks.

The hearing took less than ten minutes. This time Haluk turned around and gave the thumbs up sign. Erdal was sentenced to twenty months but was released as he'd already served the full term. The judge, however, did not pass up the opportunity to give Erdal a severe dressing down. If he re-offended they'd throw the book at him.

This time Clare's tears were those of joy. All the pent-up emotion of the last twenty months came flooding out. As they left the court building she squeezed Erdal so hard he winced, and his frail body crumpled into her embrace.

"You are free darling. Thank God. We'll go to the coast and you can recover. Then I'll take you to Tucson and we can plan our future together. I will never leave you, my love."

After Erdal's release, he and Clare had spent two months in an old stone house in the mountains overlooking the Karaburun Peninsula on the westernmost tip of Turkey's Aegean coast. Ever so slowly Erdal had regained his strength and his humanity. Clare doted on him and nurtured him back to health. She would bathe and massage him, read to him, play music cassettes for him, feed him wholesome Turkish breakfasts—warm, freshly baked bread; *beyaz peynir* (white cheese); olives; *cacik* (natural yoghurt and cucumber); *karpuz* (water melon); and copious amounts of çay (tea).

At first Erdal felt so weak that he had to use a walking stick, and he could only manage five minute strolls. But each day he was able to venture further, and before long, he was walking to and from the nearest village, which was half an hour away. En route, they would marvel at the variety of fauna and flora; gorgeous maroon and white orchids, the elegant white and yellow flecked narcissus flowers—their heavenly primrose scent floating on the breeze—the lilac colored hyacinths and green artichoke plants everywhere.

They would sit on the patio of the fish restaurant eating the best fish Clare had ever tasted in her life. *Hamsi* (anchovy) and *kalkan* (turbot) were popular local offerings. They would spend dreamy days gazing out at the sea from an intimate cove. It was a patchwork of color. Powder, royal, and steel blues were all in evidence. Four foot high bleached stone walls ringed the pebble beach. Clare loved to lie on her back and have Erdal bury her in pebbles. Their damp, smooth weight reminded her of the feeling of sliding into a cool, freshly made bed that has an excess of blankets pushing down.

In September 1997 they were married at the town hall in Izmir. Clare was expecting a rough ride but the American officials could not have been more relaxed. Erdal thought it was because the Turks had been compliant allies during the Gulf War and supported the Iraq sanctions throughout the nineties.

January 2000

Erdal lay on his bed watching his cellmate Enrique, a short, stocky, Mexican boxer, shave. As Enrique's left arm moved gently up and down, his rippling biceps tensed then loosened, creating a wave effect and his flame-colored Aztec Sun Stone tattoo also appeared to undulate. The two of them were inmates in the Tucson section of Arizona's huge State Prison Complex. As Enrique examined his lean body at length, Erdal reflected on his ability to self-implode. Fresh start, new country, the love of his life at his side; so what does he do? Gets himself a tidy little two-year prison term for drunk driving. He lost control of his car, ploughed into a bus shelter at Grant and Swan and fractured a sixty-six-year-old man's hip in the process. If the victim hadn't been drunk and in the middle of trashing the shelter it could have been far worse. The lawyers of course had had a field day. The issue of how much damage the drunk pedestrian had inflicted upon the shelter before the drunk driver finished the job off had been a tricky one to determine.

It was the guilt that was hardest to come to terms with; after all Clare had done for him, this was the way he repaid her. She had been mortified, unable to comprehend how lightning could strike twice. She blamed herself for not having seen it coming, but Erdal knew that he and he alone was culpable.

As Erdal lay back on his thin, lumpy mattress he realized how much he was missing Tucson. He liked the slow pace of life and was often highly amused by some of the Old Pueblo's quirks. In particular, he was left open-mouthed at the sight of some of the vehicles on its roads. He was repulsed by those gigantic pick-ups which had had expensive lift-kits fitted to raise their frames way above the wheels and the axle; nonetheless he was strangely mesmerized by them. And he was also seduced by the pristine big rigs with their huge steel grilles gleaming in the sunlight. Most of all, he was fascinated by the rugged, fifty-something bikers who sported grey pony tails, knee-high boots, bandanas, and mirrored Ray-Bans. Maybe he was wrong, but he assumed they must all have led colorful lives. He resolved to engage one of them in conversation when he got out.

He struck up a rapport with a hugely entertaining greeter at a Fry's supermarket. Julio was a diminutive man in his forties who was always dressed in an open-necked cream shirt, black pants, and matching black waistcoat, replete with a red Fry's logo and ID badge. He patrolled the entrance area, working the customers with ease.

"Hello Sir, Hello Madam, nice to see the two of you and each one of you. My name's Julio and I offer you service with serenity and a smile. Would you like to see our sales paper? Let me get you a cart." Factor in his bushy moustache and rat-a-tat delivery and he was every inch the Latino Groucho Marx. Erdal had always appreciated characters and there were an abundance of them in Tucson.

Erdal found a job at a woodworking firm in the warehouse district at Park and Twentieth, where he could put into practice the woodworking skills he'd learned in prison. The company made upscale custom furniture and had a mushrooming client base that included local politicians and celebrities. On one occasion Erdal's quick reaction had prevented an important client from being hit by a large block of wood. He'd been duly rewarded with a company pen and fridge magnet.

For the first year or so, he was given the most basic of tasks: sanding, planing, and hand sawing small pieces of wood. Then, they trained him to use their machinery, planer-jointers, routers, and mortisers. Erdal showed himself to be a fast learner and soon earned himself a decent pay hike. Most of the staff were perfectly friendly to him, although none of them expressed any interest in socializing with him. There was one guy, though, who was surly and never spoke to Erdal. He would sometimes train his black, bloodshot eyes on him; Erdal could sense genuine malevolence.

Erdal once asked him, "Why you not speak to me? Did I do bad things?" Stony faced and square jawed, the man finished off licking the sticky part of his rolling paper, spat out saliva mixed with tobacco on the ground at Erdal's feet, and walked away. Momentarily, Erdal imagined himself head-butting the man on the bridge of his nose, watching the blood spurt randomly out of the wound, some of it directly onto his own mouth. He could taste it, metallic and coppery, on his lips. There had been a fellow inmate in Merter who had bided his time before "accidently" bumping into Erdal in the canteen and spilling a piping hot plate of pasta all over him. Erdal was impassive, and the incident was a non-event and would be again, now. But Erdal instinctively knew that this guy would eventually strike. And sure enough, nineteen months into his employment it happened. It was short and brutal.

"Mr. Yılmaz, I am terminating your employment immediately," said Mr. Cummins, the new general manager.

"Why?" asked Erdal.

"For theft, Mr. Yılmaz. It has been brought to my attention that you have stolen one hundred dollars from petty cash. You were seen putting the money in your locker."

"I have worked here one year and a half, Mr. Cummins. You think I am suddenly not honest. Why I need one hundred dollars? My salary is good, is enough for me." *Pezvenk* (pimp), thought Erdal.

Cummins was unmoved. "Well, let's go see what's in your locker then, shall we?" Erdal knew what was coming. "It's okay Mr. Cummins. I don't need to see one hundred dollars you and your friends put in it. You think I am idiot?" Cummins feigned outrage.

"Well I'll be damned. Just what are you suggesting Mr. Yılmaz? I'd watch your step if I was you."

"I don't care about your job Mr. Cummins. You are small man. My life better without you and your spies." Erdal was out the door before the dull-witted Cummins had a chance to respond.

Clare was outraged. "I can't let this go, Erdal. Cummins is a fucker. You told me he didn't like you. All pally with that slime ball. I'm going to report them for this. I'll contact the Chamber of Commerce. Maybe I'll go to the press." Erdal massaged her shoulders. "Calm down, *canım*. It is done. Leave it alone, okay? Don't worry. I can find new job. Trust me. Maybe was time to move."

Erdal was as good as his word. In next to no time he had secured another job as a pizza delivery man for Pizza Paradiso, an independent concern at River and Campbell. The pay, minimum wage, was much less than he earned before, but the tips were decent. And Erdal liked being out and about. It was a good way for him to get to know some of Tucson's nooks and crannies. The things that Erdal saw when delivering pizza to peoples' front doors were extraordinary. He saw everything from an elderly, stark naked woman whose rose pink nails must have been at least three quarters of an inch long to a Rastafarian guy called Chicago who covered himself with chain-mail crafted from pull-tabs.

The owner, Luigi, a portly Italian-American, began to train Erdal to make pizza dough, a painstaking process which required a deceptive amount of skill. Although it wasn't something that the somewhat dour Luigi encouraged, as it was basically only a party trick, Erdal liked to practice tossing the dough at home. You cupped your hands underneath it, one slightly higher than the other, and simply flicked the wrists. He soon had Clare trying out her skills, but she just couldn't get the hang of it. The dough tended to end up stuck to the ceiling. The fourteen months that Erdal was at Paradiso were among the happiest they had spent together.

Clare had plenty of teaching work and they were living in a cozy apartment on North Fourth Street, a stone's throw away from University Boulevard. They would hang out for hours on end at Epic Café on the corner of Fourth Avenue and University. It was an art-laden, bohemian joint whose motto was "disturbing the comfortable and comforting the disturbed." You could get up close and personal with the full gamut of humankind; anarcho-syndicalists, environmentalists, bookworms, and body art exhibitionists were all represented. Clare felt blessed to live on the doorstep of a place that offered African rose tea and the best vegan cookies she'd ever tasted.

She got a buzz out of showing Erdal some of her childhood and teenage haunts; Tucson Botanical Gardens, Agua Caliente Park, and the Santa Rita Hotel and Ballroom among them. She told him about the time Gregory Peck, Cary Grant, and Clarke Gable all stayed at the Santa Rita while they were shooting a movie at the Old Tucson Studios and Peck actually rode a horse into the hotel lobby. Her parents took her there a few times and she would spend ages floating on her air mattress in the secluded courtyard pool, looking up at the thin-trunked, eighty-foot-high Washington palm trees.

Erdal's commitment to his new American life was enough to win over Linda, Clare's mother. "I admit it, I was too quick to judge him," she told Clare. "You may have fallen on your feet after all."

"I told you Mom, he's a good person and he'd do anything for me. That's a rare thing."

"Well darling, let's hope he stays true. And by the way, I also hope he keeps his earnings here for both of you to use. I keep hearing how foreigners send everything back home to their families or to invest in property."

"What's wrong with that Mom?"

"I just think they should put money back into our economy. After all, we're the ones giving them the opportunity."

"Oh come on Mom. That's their own choice, no? They pay taxes like everyone else, don't they?"

"Maybe, but I still don't like the idea that they're using us, and then they'll be outta here super fast when they feel like it."

"Very surprised you'd hold a view like that Mum."

"Well, I do my girl, so I guess you better get used to it." Clare took a deep breath and let it go. She knew herself too well. Once she embarked on a political discussion, nine out of ten times it ended badly.

And then, the proverbial bolt from the blue. Luigi was taken over by Dominos, too good an offer to turn down apparently, and they would be bringing in their own staff. Luigi was already talking about the villa he was going to build in his home town of Rimini, on Italy's Adriatic coast. Erdal would have to visit, and Luigi would show him where Federico Fellini was born. From that moment on the gods appeared to turn their backs on Clare and Erdal; the good karma that had enveloped them for several years evaporated. Her teaching work dried up, and he couldn't find a job that interested him—he certainly wasn't prepared to take an entry-level position at a Quick Mart or a 7-11. They couldn't afford to keep their Fourth Street place and had to take a basement apartment at Stone and Drachmann.

Linda was diagnosed with breast cancer. She became heavily reliant on Clare and all Clare and Erdal's spare cash spare cash went towards the medical bills. Erdal's father had a major heart attack and he didn't have the money to go and see him.

"For God's sake Erdal. Why are you being so stubborn? What was wrong with that job at the paper company? It wasn't bad money."

It was a tiny bit over minimum Clare, and I must stay whole day in same room in basement. I can do better." Clare was exasperated.

"And the YMCA job? What's your excuse for that one?"

"Don't say excuse like that. It is not nice. I don't like YMCA job, okay. Mainly cleaning and sometimes help in swimming pool. Money is bad also. I know what I can do. Why you panic like this? I never saw that before."

"Why are you so relaxed? We have no money Erdal. You understand that, right?"

"We have little money, not 'no' money. I know. But what about you? You could try something else apart teaching, but you refuse. You are stubborn one, no?"

"Come on, Erdal. I already explained my reasons. But let me explain one more time. I have a qualification, and there is such a huge difference between what I can earn from teaching and what I will make doing other jobs. I need to focus all my energy on finding a teaching job."   "Okay, maybe you are right but why you not sell this car and buy cheap one? And why you not sell the bracelet? What is *your* excuse now?"

"You don't know what it's like selling a car in this country. You just don't know who you're dealing with. I don't feel strong enough right now to be messed around by every John Doe in town. And if I buy a car on the cheap it's bound to cost me a ton of money in the long run. And as for the bracelet, shame on you for even suggesting it. You know my granny gave it to me. It's the only thing of hers I've got, and I will never sell it. It's priceless, simple as that."

"Ok, I never say anything, you know the best always, no point to speak."

There were many such exchanges, and each time the bitterness increased. On the day of the accident they'd had another blazing row. Clare wanted Erdal to ask his relatives in Turkey for some money, but he was too proud to consider it. He'd stormed off after downing several whiskies at home, and that was when he'd had the accident.

When Erdal came home he'd served nineteen months. It was as though he was present in body but not in soul. He looked immaculate physically; his well-developed pectorals were a testament to his three-hundred-push-ups-per-day regime. But he was withdrawn and monosyllabic.   What was wrong? He couldn't be specific. He wasn't proud of himself. He was having difficulty picturing the future. Maybe he'd go back to Turkey. Enough time had gone by. He had some business ideas. He had a criminal record now. And everyone knew that having one of those in America was tantamount to having one arm tied permanently behind your back. "Honey, I know you're down and I understand. Honestly, I really do. But don't do anything hasty. You know I can't leave Mom right now, don't you? We'll get through this. We've been through a lot worse, right?" Clare said that night, as they savored their favorite Rakı. "Maybe love, maybe. I just feel the need to move. To breathe. To live again. I can go to the homeland and start preparing a future for us. We have an expression in Turkey; *Yaşanan herşey bir tarafa bırakıp, hayata yeniden başlamak.* Means that we want fresh start in life." Erdal got up from his chair and knelt down in front of Clare. He laid his head in her lap and didn't move for a very long time.

The Gambian Dreamer

Dawda Jammeh was so deep in thought that he did not even notice the white fishnet stockinged transvestite who sat down next to him. As the bus headed north along Oracle Road, he saw neither the smiling, twenty feet tall, green and yellow sky puppet, flapping in the wind like a demonic disco-dancer, nor the brawl between two scrawny, inebriated women in their sixties which was taking place on a K-Mart forecourt. One was attempting to wallop the other with a bunch of celery.

Mind you, Dawda had always had a propensity to daydream, sometimes at the most inappropriate moments. One such occasion had happened when, at the age of twelve, his father had left him in charge of fifteen cattle in their pen on the family farm in the Lower Saloum district of Gambia's Central River Division. While Dawda dozed off, as he visualized himself as a prince being transported in a carriage full of beglittered, yellow mermaids along the banks of the River Gambia, the cattle were stolen. When his father returned an hour later, Dawda could offer no explanation as to their disappearance.

Perhaps it was the sheer ordinariness of Dawda's upbringing on a cattle farm that encouraged him to spend countless hours in the world of make-believe. The most remarkable thing that had ever happened to him as a child was fishing a rusty air rifle out of the river and, minutes later, accidently blasting a hole in the wall of his neighbor's mud hut. His father had been forced to give the neighbor three cattle to appease him. From then on, there were some villagers who believed that Dawda possessed special powers. He was occasionally asked to participate in libation ceremonies for the ancestors.

Everything changed on the day he attended the Friendship Stadium in

Banjul at the age of thirteen. It was his first ever visit to the capital, Banjul, and his best friend, Julius, had invited him to see Gambia under eighteens play South Africa under eighteens in the African championships. Dawda was awestruck. He had only ever seen single-story, wood and mud dwellings. Now, he was inside a huge concrete structure that housed twenty thousand people. Dawda did not see the drab, grey, vertical edifices and green and white Gambian flags that others saw. Instead, he imagined a glorious, walled city floating in space, protected by green-winged creatures whose huge ears flapped gently in the wind like palm fronds but who had dainty, pink, human feet.

Dawda was captivated by the match and the roar of the crowd. He paid no attention to the intricacies of football itself and had no idea what the score was. All he saw were little dwarves prancing around a field while trying to avoid being hit by a white circular object.

After it was all over, Julius's father spoke to Dawda in a serious manner.

"Dawda Jammeh, you have been chosen by the ancestors to be the vehicle for communication between Banjul and the United States. It has been foretold that you are the one to bring us riches, that you are the one whose head will not be twisted by idle promises, that you are the one who will not forget his own abundant soil, that you are the one who will always remain steadfast in the face of exploiters. What say you, chosen one?"

Dawda did not understand. "What is the United States?"

"It is a land of plenty, a trading paradise where everything has a price. It is there that you will learn to barter with the white man and feel as comfortable in his world as you do in ours."

"But, sir, I am only waiting to learn of our own customs and of city life in Banjul."

"There is time a plenty for that, boy. For now, you will go far away and with your parents' blessing."

And so it was, that at the tender age of fourteen, a young dreamer from Gambia was dispatched to the biggest marketplace on earth.

Wherever Dawda was he was elsewhere. That is to say, his mind and his body were worlds apart. Daydreaming or being "a million miles away" was the norm rather than the exception for Dawda. In America, Dawda was told he had an affliction known as ADD, which apparently stood for Attention Deficit

Disorder. They said he did not pay attention to anything for very long and did not follow instructions from grownups properly, which meant that he could not hope to develop normally as a person. While that was not a good thing, he was not as badly off as many other children who were hyperactive, which meant that they just could not stop talking and moving around. Sometimes, they would say embarrassing things in public, such as "Why is that man so fat?" or "Why don't you have any hair on your head?" In Africa, however, on account of his special status, Dawda's tendency to daydream was usually seen in a positive light. It was felt that he was in communication with the ancestors who were probably imparting to him some home truths. normally not follow instructions from grown-ups properlyey would say embarassing to develop properly as a person.

As soon as Dawda arrived in Tucson, where he was to be taken under the wing of the feisty octogenarian, Uncle Pious, he fell in love with the Saguaro cactus on sight. "What are these?" he said to himself. "Have I died and gone to heaven?" The gentle giants with the saggy arms became his best friends. Only with them did he feel comfortable sharing his innermost thoughts, for they were old and wise and knew how to keep a secret. They taught him to be patient; you could not run before you could walk. They had seen all there was to see, and they would teach him to be wise and also to be modest. He was sure of it from the very beginning.

Uncle Pious was a softly spoken, 6' 8" Senegalese man, who was never seen without a pork-pie hat, dark glasses, a black leather waistcoat, and a Malacca cane with an exquisite ivory handle carved to show dog and horse heads. For some four decades, he'd overseen the transition to American life of a succession of hand-picked West African boys who were to form the vanguard of an entrepreneurial middle class. The idea was for them to return to Africa later in life to impart to their compatriots their finely-honed, street-level skills. "You are ever safe with me, boys. Your Uncle Pious will show you how to turn molasses into malachite and licorice into lapis," he would say to his charges. "Us Africans are as wise as the owl, as cunning as the fox, as graceful as the gazelle, and as nimble as the squirrel. We are coming, boys. The world just doesn't know it yet."

Arguably, as counter-intuitive as an ex-con who wishes he was back inside or a freed colonial subject who harks back nostalgically to the days when his country was under the yoke of the colonial power, Ayesha often yearned for the days when she was living under a blue United Nations tarpaulin in the Hagadera refugee camp, one of three camps which are part of the huge Dadaab complex. Built twenty years ago to house some ninety thousand but now teeming with nearly four hundred thousand, it is situated sixty miles from Kenya's border with her parents' Somali homeland. It was where she was born, and all she'd ever known until, at the age of eight, the UN resettled her family and fifty other Somali families to Chicago.

Ayesha never settled in Chicago; it was too cold, too inhospitable, too alienating. They—her mother, Fatima, sister, Maryan, brother, Mahad, cousin Tawfiq, and aunt Warsan were forever being shunted around from one drafty, dull apartment to another. Yes, they had enough food, electricity, running water, toilets, beds, furniture, and television, all of which was good. But somehow, Ayesha was uncomfortable. There was something about the white man's house that made Ayesha feel claustrophobic. Maybe it was the standard box-shaped rooms or the whitewashed walls. She couldn't put her finger on it. All she knew was that she'd felt at ease in their hotchpotch mud, bamboo, thatch, and plastic dwelling. Although it was cramped and leaky, it had been home to the family for ten years, and they'd made it surprisingly cozy. There were rugs made out of cardboard, string and acacia leaves, candles, and colorful drapes made out of strips of discarded fabric.

She missed the camaraderie at the camp, the friendly faces, people like Mohamed the bottle collector, Saud the juggler, and Yusuf the soothsayer. And then there was her best friend, Safiya, from whom she was inseparable. They did everything together, whether it be collecting firewood, playing in the pond, hula-hooping, or just sharing their dreams about what they'd do if they ever got out of the camp. Both of them had their hearts set on being hairdressers or beauticians, and they used to give each other hairdos and henna tattoos. Ayesha missed Safiya so much it hurt. She cried every day and prayed she would see her again.

After four years of wrapping herself up like a Russian doll in the Windy City, Ayesha and her family were relocated to Tucson. Once again, she found herself at the sharp end of nature's wrath, this time beneath Arizona's destructive desert sun. But this was no sand-filled Saharan mono-universe, rather it was a bountiful basin carved into the Sonoran desert, straddling majestic sky islands and multiple eco-systems. Our ancestors tilled its soil four thousand years ago, appreciating its raw, savage, almost ineffable beauty. As she cast her eyes on the snowy tips of Tucson's mountain ranges, the Santa Catalinas to the north, the Santa Ritas to the southeast, the Rincons to the east, and the Tucson mountains to the west, Ayesha felt herself floating in the stratosphere. "What is this place God has sent me to? Is this a staircase to heaven? I think I will live here and die here," she said to herself.

"That's right, Ayesha. Lie back on me. I'll support you, my love. Good girl. Now gently paddle with your legs. That's it, you're doing great." Heather, a volunteer with Maendeleo, a refugee support group, was helping to teach her to swim. The pool at Catalina High School was full of African children and a mixture of American and European volunteers. Black and white on blue, smiles and shrieks, wet bodies entangled, pure unmediated human contact, beautiful color-blind bonding. One boy of about twelve stood by the side of the pool and wept, his whole body shuddering as he did so. Heather found it a haunting sight. Maybe he was one of the many Africans who had had to endure the terrifying ordeal of crossing crocodile infested waters when fleeing for their lives, she thought. One girl, giggling with a mixture of excitement and apprehension, blurted out, "Oh, my God, am I going to die right here?"

Maendeleo specialized in resettlement of United Nations refugees, which involved finding housing, organizing welfare and education, and ensuring refugees had the correct papers. Its founder was Shirley Masters, an actress turned activist. She was a one-off, a force of nature, who was not afraid to ruffle feathers. Shirley had fought with Refugee Relief and Arizona Integration Service, Tucson's principal refugee resettlement agencies, more times than most people had eaten fish tacos. "If your lot did what you say you're going to do in your glossy brochures I wouldn't have to keep bugging you," she'd say to them. She knew they were underfunded and overworked but still felt compelled to keep them on their toes. In her eyes, it was crucial that they met their responsibilities to educate refugees as to their rights and to collaborate effectively with their fellow stakeholders in the community. Shirley, the envelope pusher, the glass half-full merchant, often irritated the hell out of them. But they knew she was indispensable to the refugee community in Tucson and respected her for that.

"Who is this sleeping boy? How very strange to be sleeping in the playground at this early time in the morning. Most of us only woke up less than two hours ago, not so?" said Ayesha.

"Oh, that's dozy Dawda. Don't worry about him. He sleeps for Gambia at the Olympics," said Abdullah, a lanky, fourteen year old Somali boy with frizzy hair.

They all roared with laughter.

"Ssssshhh. We don't want to wake him, do we?" said Yohan, a sixteen year old Congolese boy, who was the drummer in an African band.

"Yohan. Let me tell you. This boy would not be woken even by the earthquake. Some of us were downtown some weeks ago, near railway line. We were relaxing and Dawda dropped off to sleep. Then the cargo train came. Oh my God, the rumble and the horn were very, very loud. Everything was vibrating for a few minutes and still this boy did not wake up. Can you imagine living in that area? It would be terrible." Abdullah shuffled his worry beads and patted his hair so that it was momentarily depressed before springing back up like a sponge ball. They all looked down at Dawda for another minute or so before moving off to see what livelier activities were taking place.

"I met you last Monday." Ayesha approached Dawda as they waited outside the classroom where their math lesson was about to start.

"Cannot be. I am sure I would have remembered you."

"You were asleep in the playground," said Ayesha.

Dawda laughed. "Really! That is a little embarrassing. Hope I was not snoring."

"No, you were not snoring, but I did notice one thing which was strange."

"Oh really?"

"Yes, you kept blinking."

"I was probably dreaming. I always do that when I dream."

"What do you dream about?"

"Well, let me see. I dream about flying inside a cactus, about riding around

91

the White House on an elephant with Prince Shiny Teeth Barak, and returning to Gambia with a wife, six children, twenty-four humming birds, a Gila Monster, and a Javelina."

"A Javelina, you're crazy. They are sooooo ugly and smelly."

"I don't agree. I think they are quite sweet and gentle, and they look so strange, especially their thin legs. Anyway, your turn to tell me what you dream about."

"Umm, not sure. Umm, okay, I know. I dream of having my own restaurant and cooking wonderful African dishes like Fufu and Kuli-Kuli. The restaurant would have a big painting of a colorful African dance and lots of wooden masks."

"Sounds great. Hey, I just realized. I don't even know your name."

"I'm Ayesha. They call me the snail because I do everything very slowly. Americans are always in a hurry, not so? I always tell them: slow down, you are still young, relax, and let things happen when they are meant to happen. Me, where I lived before I came here, there was no such thing as being in a hurry. Maybe only once we ran, into the bush when there was a rumor a group of gunmen were coming."

"Together we are a dozy snail, right? A good combo, I think."

Dawda and Ayesha loved to hang out downtown, in and around the Joel D. Valdez Library, The Court House, El Presidio Park, the Ronstadt bus station-named after the influential Tucson family of the singer, Linda Ronstadt- and Hotel Congress. They liked the mixture of modern buildings—mirrored, rectangular skyscrapers alongside hybrid, creatively clad, multi-angled structures—the more classical domed structures and the funky red and yellow metal installation sculptures. "It's such fun, so many shapes and sizes. Maybe some Africans were helping them," or words to that effect was how they described the architectural mélange. And they dug the downtown vibe. "It's so nice around here. People are very friendly and what what. You can slope along without any rush," said Ayesha.

Dawda concurred. "It's true. The best thing is you can meet very odd people, who always tell you funny stories. I once met a guy who had three feet long grey hair and bright red shoes. He just kept on dancing, never stayed still. He was carrying a very old, small, leather case which was full of old stamps. He told me he inherited them from his granny twenty years before and was saving them for a rainy day."

Yohan dangled some keys in front of Abdullah, Dawda, and Ayesha. "Road trip guys. What do you say?" He was beaming from ear to ear.

"This boy is so happy. Did you win twenty dollars on those scratchy cards?" asked Ayesha.

"No, no, silly, it's much better than that. My uncle took the shuttle to Phoenix, and he said I could use his car. It's a Nissan Sentra, yellow color."

"You have a license?" enquired Abdullah.

"Oh man, do I look stupid to you? Of course I have a license, a G Class one. I'm over sixteen, remember. So, who's in, who's out?"

Yohan and Abdullah were up front and the dozy snail duo in the rear. They were cruising along the I-10 towards Bisbee. The windows were down, and the strong through breeze sounded like a kite flapping. They were listening to African grooves and munching on some trail mix. "We're gliding along like African cheetah friends. The force is with us. Can you feeeeeel it, guys?"

"Yeeees, we can feeeeel it, Yohan."

"Yes, but can you really feeeeeeel it?" Yohan was drunk with happiness. Not only was he driving a car long distance for the first time, he'd also been accepted by Pima Community College to do a carpentry course. Things were definitely looking up.

"Hey, Yohan, maybe I sell your uncle car seat covers, furry brown ones, nice and cheap," said Dawda.

"You sell seat covers? Since when?" said Yohan.

"I've got a few stocks and stuffs in my garage. From time to time, I sell sell buy buy. Small small, you know."

"Wow, he may be dozy but he's the darkest horse," said Abdullah.

"What a boy he is, this Gambian. Always has surprises under the sleeve." Ayesha nudged Dawda affectionately and they got into a rough and tumble. The four high-spirited Africans were headed for Bisbee, a quaint frontier town in Southern Arizona that, some one hundred and twenty five years earlier, had been one of the foremost mining towns in the world. Millions of pounds of gold and copper were produced there, and silver, zinc, and lead were also extracted from the depths of the mineral-rich, Mule Mountains. At the entrance to the town, they passed the now disused open-pit copper mines, circumscribed by ridged lavender, mustard, and faintly turquoise rock formations.

They were all agreed that Bisbee was a special place: the one thousand stair climb up into the hills on which old houses appeared to be precariously perched, the ghost tour, the art galleries, the steep, narrow, winding streets, and, the crowning glory, the Mini Museum of the Bizarre. About the size of a walk-in wardrobe, it was full of very weird oddities; a mummified cat, a double-headed squirrel, a mold of a yeti footprint, and a Fiji Mermaid, which had the head of a monkey and the torso of a fish. "Oh, my God. I'm going to have nightmares after seeing all those scary things. Can you imagine working there? Must be the worst job in the world, even worse than standing in the street for hours holding a car wash sign," said Yohan.

"I prefer that job than being a leaf-blower. Most pointless ever job and noisy too," opined Abdullah.

Dawda and Ayesha both saw it differently, considering it to be a fun job.

"Look out, Yohan," yelled Abdullah. "There is blockage coming up, look, there is a bar fence."

Yohan was speaking to a friend on his cell phone about basketball and had lost concentration. He screeched to a halt a mere ten or eleven feet from the Border Patrol checkpoint, one of many seemingly ad-hoc checkpoints which can crop up anywhere within twenty or thirty miles of the Mexican border.

"Shit, this is somewhat of a mistake, Yohan. These men are pointing guns at us," said Abdullah.

Meanwhile, Yohan was still on the phone. "I must go now, Mohamud. We reached some sort of checkpoint."

As the bright yellow car approached at a worryingly fast pace, the four uniformed officers instinctively reached for their firearms and squatted down into combat mode. For at least thirty seconds after the car stopped nothing happened. The officers then stood up and took two or three steps forward. "Everyone out the car, hands on your heads," shouted one of them who was both pectorally enhanced and follically challenged. As soon as they got a clearer look at the kids, the officers relaxed and put their guns away. But they were still very pissed. "What the hell were you thinking? You could get yourself killed doing that kind of thing," the same guy told Yohan.

"I am very sorry, sir. I made a mistake, lost my concentration. I will make sure it never happens again."

"IDs please, everyone."

Yohan provided his Arizona driving license; Abdullah handed over a crumpled copy of his photoless i94 visa, an oddly unofficial looking document for one so crucial to refugees. "I've seen more official looking papers inside a Rice Crispies packet," was a stock Shirley observation. Ayesha and Dawda produced their green cards. Yohan and Abdullah were clearly causing the officials concern. They quizzed them as to their status.

"We're African refugees, sir. We came here with the United Nations and we live in Tucson," said Abdullah.

The youngsters waited nervously in the car while phone calls were made. The bombshell of an outcome was that Ayesha and Dawda were free to go and Yohan and Abdullah were to be detained. The officers would follow Yohan for the seven miles back to Bisbee where he could park his car and from where the other two could get someone to collect them.

For a week nobody knew where they were. Refugee Relief and Arizona Integration Service, who were responsible for Yohan and Abdullah respectively, suspected that they were being held at the notorious Eloy Immigration Detention Center, a privately run establishment with a record of detainee abuse and about as much transparency as a reclusive tadpole in a frog pond, but kept hitting a brick wall when they sought information from both Border Patrol and Immigration and Customs Enforcement (ICE). When they finally located them, they were indeed at Eloy, some fifty miles north of Tucson, but had apparently spent four days at a facility in Texas. ICE had already initiated deportation proceedings against both the boys on the grounds that they had failed to apply in time for their permanent resident status, commonly referred to as a green card. UN refugees are given i94 visas, which run for three hundred and sixty-five days, when they first arrive. They have to make such applications prior to the expiry of the i94.

The boys were incarcerated for eighteen weeks, the first time in their lives they'd ever been locked up. "The law is all important in this country. You broke it, plain and simple. We gave you a chance to live in the land of the free but you blew it, guys. Sorry, but you will have to go back to Africa." The six foot seven inch, two hundred sixty pound immigration officer could see the fear on the faces of Yohan and Abdullah.

"But Sir, we are not criminals. All we are asking for is safety in your great country," said Abdullah.

"I'm sorry young man. But life can be cruel. We don't always get second chances. Try to come back again in a few years. I'm sure your attorney will advise you."

"Sir, are you very certain that this new life we are so blessed to have been given by the Almighty will now be taken from us?" asked Yohan.

"Yes, I am sure. I have seen many Africans sent back. None of them ever seem to think it's going to happen, even when they are boarding the plane."

"How could this happen? Maybe we were complacent. All we wanted was to improve ourselves. To give back to America. We didn't think about our papers." Yohan began to cry. The officer left the room.

Yohan and Abdullah were both unhappy at Eloy. Yohan suffered from bad acid indigestion and was always asking the officers for some Tums. He was given a single packet every three or four weeks. Abdullah had suffered from migraines for several years and would beg them for strong painkillers. All they managed was a handful of aspirin, which they brought at the same time as Yohan's Tums. Sometimes, the heating was ramped up, and the boys would sweat for hours on end. On other occasions it was so cold they felt like they were living in a cold storage unit. They asked for books or magazines to read. Nothing for a month and then they were brought a magazine called *Home and Garden* and a book entitled *Fundamentals of Statistics*. Texas had also been awful. When they arrived, they were kept in a frozen cell with sixteen others, all Americans, for more than fifteen hours. They got one glass of water and a peanut butter sandwich and were only permitted to visit the rest room one time.

Ayesha escaped the boys' fate because she had been taken under Shirley's wing. Shirley had organized some Maendeleo green card application sessions and had liaised with Refugee Relief and Arizona Integration Service when they conducted their own, much larger, ones. Whether it was due to the fact that they charged individual refugees seventy dollars for doing the application—there were often as many as ten people within an extended family—or because the message had not filtered down to everyone, was unclear. But Yohan, Abdullah, and a dozen or so others had fallen through the net.

Shirley took Ayesha to visit the boys, and she immediately managed to lift their spirits. Her thirty second cameos were legendary. First an improvised African dance involving shuffle steps and the odd quick darting movement from a crouched position. And then some meditation. Eyes shut while Shirley chanted the Buddhist Om mantra and the others then joined in. They were soon engulfed in a wave of warm, vibratory transcendence. Yohan and Abdullah found themselves laughing for the first time since the day of the arrest. By the time the security grunt ran over to break up the party, the aura of positivity continued to swamp all of his opposing vibes.

Shirley explained to the boys that nobody in reality gets deported for late green card applications. "It's all just a charade so they can justify their own existence. They are just doing what the Feds want them to do. They need to detain a whole bunch of folks so they can use up the budget they get for signing up to a Homeland Security program after 9-11. Most of the officers don't even know the difference between UN refugees, undocumented immigrants, and asylees. It's criminals and terrorists they're really interested in. You boys are what's called 'collateral damage.'" Abdullah and Yohan looked blank. "Collateral damage just means you get punished just for being in the wrong place at the wrong time. It's rotten luck."

One day, after swimming, Shirley and Heather took Ayesha and a bunch of refugee kids out for lunch to a Jack in the Box. Chicken and fries with coleslaw and onion rings were hugely popular within Tucson's African community. It was the kind of quintessentially American food they loved, other favorites being Big Macs, sixty-four ounce buckets of popcorn, thirty-two ounce cups of soda, and Dunkin' Donuts. They found the fast-food concept fascinating, the size of everything and the way every meal was identical. Not like in Africa, they would say, where every day the dish you create will always be a bit different.

Some of the children, Ayesha included, lived at the Cherokee Apartments, a low income, mid-town, housing project. Shirley and Heather watched as an argument broke out in the parking lot over the distribution of a bag of candy bars. Three girls began kicking and pulling each other's hair. Shirley soon calmed them all down and divided up the goodies. A couple of heavily tattooed working-class American teenagers wearing cookie-cutter baggy jeans, Nike air force pumps, and reversed baseball caps strolled by. Both were smoking. One of them was carrying a boom-box and the other, a crate of Budweisers. They nodded towards Shirley and Heather. One of the refugee boys ran over to them and tried to mimic their fluid, shuffling walk. Everybody yelped with laughter. Shirley smelled marijuana in the air. For the refugees, those guys are the paradigm of American youth, she thought.

Ayesha lived with her five family members in a shabby, three-room apartment. They had a problem with the landlord who was threatening to evict them because they'd asked him to deal with a cockroach infestation. Apparently, the roaches weren't there before the family moved in so it must have been caused by something they did. Shirley knew all about the scare tactics of slum landlords, and this particular one was about to be shaken out of his smugness by a blast from Maendeleo Masters.

"Can you help us, Aunty?" asked Ayesha.

"You better believe it, my sweet. This man thinks he can get away with avoiding his responsibilities, but we have to teach him a lesson, you see. All of us have responsibilities that we have to meet. Otherwise people are harmed and society breaks down. We can't have that, can we, my sweet?"

"No, Aunty, of course we ca …."

Shirley picked Ayesha up and swung her round and round.

"Aaaaaah. Aunty, put me down. I just ate too much food."

The Bisbee Four were together for the first time since that fateful day. They hugged each other, they laughed and cried, and they shared some of their innermost feelings. Yohan hadn't been able to take up his place at college and he felt angry about it. There was a long waiting list, and it would probably be a year before he could get back into a class. "Every time I am close to doing a positive thing, something bad happens. For me, I am so near but always so far. I remember even in the camp they called me the very nearly boy. If we were waiting in line for food from UN it would finish just when I reached the front. If they needed six boys to collect wood and then receive a cup of juice I was number seven, if they wanted eleven boys for a football team I was number twelve. Even the girls would say to me, "I like you, but I like that boy a little bit more." He sighed deeply and looked up to the heavens.

"But here you are, in the land of plenty, telling your story. Do not despair brother Yohan, you are a fighter who never gives up. For sure you will sometimes meet with bad luck, but finally you will make it. I have seen how you can saw a piece of wood. One day you will build your own house. You are proud like an African should be, and I am ever sure you will be rewarded," said Dawda.

Yohan's frown turned into a smile, and they all started clapping and hollering spontaneously.

"Boy, he can talk, the sleepy one," said Ayesha. "But what is this country we live in? Really, just what is it? Is it truly the best country in the world, as us refugees believe? What is it they say? The land of the free. Maybe we should say the land of the nearly free. What happened to Yohan and Abdullah shocked me. Everything can change so quickly for us. I think we must be more careful, more thoughtful about life, look more closely at the details than others. God has sent us a warning and we have to listen to him." She put her hands together, rested the tips of her fingers on her lips, and looked up to the heavens.

"Ayesha is right. I feel different after being in prison. I had such fear when I was inside. Even more than the fear I remember when I was running from Mogadishu when I was four years old, when my brother was slaughtered in front of my eyes. That will never leave me and this will also never leave me. I was sure they were going to send me back to the camp. I told one uniform: 'Kill me right now, I cannot go back.' I could see how he loved his power, how he can do anything to keep it. That frightened me. Are we not all human? Is our blood not red? Maybe this can help me for the rest of my life. I can be relaxed, but I will always make sure I have my eyes and ears open and my mind alert. In twenty years, maybe they will call me 'Always alert Abdullah.'" He giggled and the others giggled too. Then he crossed his hands, placed them on his chest, and looked up to the heavens.

"I have been lucky in my life. I have never known hardship or fear like all of you have. But those who are wiser than me have separated me from my family, and they are the ones who will decide when I can see them again. I can only pray that my mother and father are still living when that day comes. This is the life that the Almighty and the ancestors have planned for me. I will follow this path and try every day to do some good. We are blessed to live here in safety, knowing we can fill our bellies daily and sleep soundly. If we can show the Yankees that we Africans are to be reckoned with this will be good for the future generations. Let me first meet Barack Hussein, and together I am sure we will work out the right strategy. Maybe if I ask him nicely he will show me his birth certificate."

The four of them all fell about laughing. Dawda snorted, then fell silent and looked up to the heavens.

The Lawyer And The Lapdancers

Morris Hertzelberger liked to have lunch now and then at Tucson's eighty-year old Arizona Inn hotel. Its fourteen acres of manicured greenery provided the perfect desert oasis. The Inn, as he referred to it, always brought back happy memories as he and his wife, Barbara, had spent a romantic weekend there early on in their courtship. Often, when something good happened, Hertzelberger would go there for a celebratory drink. On this occasion, he'd unexpectedly received an annuity of six thousand dollars from his secret life insurance plan that not even his wife knew about. After all, what was the good of a secret life if you did not have a secret income stream to support it? Hmm, Alicia or Lauren? He mulled it over for a minute or so. He texted Alicia: "Got five thousand to burn. Fancy a few days in Miami at a luxury resort?"   The reply came in within ten seconds: "Yes, baby."

Hertzelberger developed an immediate erection. Before it had died down, a plump woman approached his table and said "I know I know you."

"I know I know you too," he said. "Why don't you join me and we'll see if we can work it out." It turned out the woman was Elizabeth Goldman, who'd been at Hertzelberger's Bar Mitzvah, forty-two years ago. She'd moved to New England and recently returned to Tucson after a thirty-seven year absence. "It's such a vortex, this place. Sucks everyone back in the end," said Hertzelberger.

"You're so right, Morris. Very well put" Elizabeth smiled at her old friend. "You've hardly changed at all, you know. Did I ever tell you you were the first boy I ever had a crush on?"

"Er, Morris. Morris. Are you with us, dear boy?" Hertzelberger had been so bored by the debate around which venue to hold the firm's Christmas lunch at that he allowed his mind to wander. At the exact moment that Arnold Zeff was trying to attract his attention, Hertzelberger was lusting after Alicia and dreaming of lounging by a Miami swimming pool with her. He just could not wait to see all those losers gawking at her, wracked with envy. That scenario would be as close to nirvana as he could imagine.

"Yes, yes, I'm all ears. Sorry, guys, I was thinking ahead to the small matter of how we're going to tackle the liability insurance issue."

"Ataboy! That's the Morris we know and love," said Arnold. "Always one step ahead of us mere mortals."

"Don't make him even more big-headed, Arnold. I don't believe a word of it anyway. He was probably thinking about what to buy Barbara for a silver wedding present," opined Frank Peterson, the sole gentile on the board.

At his spacious home in the exclusive Foothills district and in his classy downtown office, Hertzlberger spent many hours reflecting on his addiction to Curves Cabaret, an "exotic dancing" establishment at the southern end of the seedy side of Tucson. "What the hell has gotten into me?" he would say to himself. "Nothing has ever gripped me to this extent and I've tried everything that's out there"—an assertion, of course, whose truth strained to fill the narrow confines of Hertzelberger's entirely correct, proper, and mundane life. A happily married man of fifty-one with two teenage children, he was also a successful attorney—wills and testaments, with a side practice in real estate law—and a reliable pillar of the city's Jewish community.   Hertzelberger did have, he was convinced, a certain "way with women," which had always tempted him to "wilder" experiences, "beyond the pale" as it were (the employment of the cliché automatically prompting him to think that few other people would know its origins as a reference to a geographical corridor running between Poland and Catherine the Great's Russia where Jews were permitted to live). But until fairly recently, he had hardly ever given in to these temptations. Why he was, all of a sudden, struggling to rein himself in was something he asked himself a great deal of the time. It was certainly something to do with the excitement generated by being a bad boy. But he had yet to come up with a convincing answer.

Despite being a very ordinary looking man—short, balding, and bespectacled—or perhaps partly on account of this or how he handled his ordinariness—he carefully cultivated a gentle manner and an unflappable courtesy with women. As a result, he found that at Curves many of the most attractive dancers stopped by his padded seat and cocktail table in front of the pole-dancing stage, knelt down, and promised him special favors in exchange for ten dollars. With this encouragement, in his own mind, playing away from home, he reflected a tad guiltily, came easily if not naturally to him.

In part because he was, he felt, a complicated man, it was far too simplistic to attribute his visits to Curves to libido alone. After all, if it was just a question of satisfying primal and illicit sexual urges, as he knew from office or late-night web surfing, there was no shortage of ladies of the night or masseuses who specialized in happy endings in Tucson. And a clean 60-minute transaction for an agreed fee tended to be far easier on the pocket than the altogether more complex arrangements that pertained to Curves. Hertzlberger concluded that his obsession—not too strong a word—was an elemental infatuation with the fairer sex, with the female form in all its glory. Nothing inspired him more than pure, youthful, feminine beauty. He liked to think himself as a connoisseur of art and recognized the bare body of a woman and the way she exhibited herself as a matter of aesthetics. No more, no less. He loved nothing more than to be in close proximity to the velvety flesh of a young woman, whether in the form of a living person or a work of art.

In tandem with the Curves addiction, indeed a corollary of it, was Hertzleberger's addiction to texting. Sex and texting. Two for the price of one, must be good, he reflected. "So what happens is that after you meet one of the girls, if you like each other you exchange cell phone numbers or, at the very least, you give your number and get promised a text soon. When they interested in seeing you they text and vice-versa. This is the girls' way of networking and building up a client base," was how Hertzleberger described it to his best friend, Jeff Rosenbaum.

"Just wanna run away with you to a desert island," was what he found himself texting to Marie at 10:43 p.m. on a Monday night in his en suite bathroom, while his wife lay in bed. "If I come down to Nogales, will you hang with me, baby?" is what he found himself texting to Jenny immediately after the Marie text. And post-text he would hold his breath as he waited anxiously for a reply. The longer it took for the reply to arrive the less likelihood that it ever would was something he discovered very early on. The sheer joy when the reply came in, particularly if it was favorable, gave him such a buzz. The only thing he had to look out for was the phone bill once a month because he certainly did not want Barbara sniffing around the text message part of the bill.

"Good afternoon, sir. Would you like to buy one of our new 2010 calendars? It's twenty bucks and you get free entry for a whole year."

"It's okay, thanks, I think I'll pass," Hertzleberger replied automatically, even as he was thinking that he would in fact quite like to buy one. Why do we humans often say the exact opposite of what we would actually like to say was a question he sometimes posed to himself when he was in one of his reflective moods. Because Hertzleberger did like to ruminate from time to time on the human condition, the older he got, the more he felt himself gravitating towards a more internal existence. He had discovered the esoteric path rather late in life and was very pleased to have done so. He liked to mull things over in his own head and come up with the answers to his own questions.

Lucas, a young, good-looking guy, with the longest sideburns Hertzelberger had ever seen, worked as a greeter/security guy at the entrance. His relaxed, happy-go-lucky personality was attractive and made him popular, not least with the fairer sex. For someone who was supposedly down on his luck, Lucas cut a surprisingly upbeat figure.

"I can tear a jet plane engine apart and put it back together again," said Lucas matter-of-factly. Hertzleberger was intrigued.

"I bet you're wondering what I'm doing here working for $5.25 an hour plus tips, don't you?"

"Sure, I was just about to ask you," said Hertzleberger.

"Well, I did time for beating up on four guys, put them all in the hospital. I do martial arts you see. I broke up a fight between my girl and these other girls, and their boyfriends all piled in. Now I gotta wait like five years before I can wipe the slate clean. Sucks, man."

"That is all very unfortunate, young man, but at least you've got time on your side, and I can think of worse places to work than in here."

Hertzleberger extended his arm and, rather like a conductor acknowledging his orchestra, swung it dramatically through 180 degrees.

Hertzelberger loved to sit and watch the girls as they worked the room. He loved the way they seemed to glide along and never ceased to be amazed at how well they coped with six inch heels. He remembered when he had worn clogs in the 1970s. Their heels had been one or two inches high and, even then, he had struggled to stay upright. Hertzelberger loved people gazing and had always enjoyed hanging out in coffee houses. But this was very different. It was not the run-of-the-mill watching the world go by type of gazing. Rather, it felt to him like he was an aesthete indulging in a hedonistic extravaganza. His eagle eye drank in every detail on every girl. The multifarious tattoos in particular, fascinated him—you could count the ones without them on the fingers of one hand—the body piercing—the mini-chains suspended from the navel were his favorite although he was also partial to the tongue studs—the array of outfits, anything from single or two-piece bikinis to spandex boob tubes to fishnet stockings. There was one girl who had a tattoo on her right shoulder which consisted of six words: "Trust No Dick. Fear No Bitch." Another had one of a sphinx moth on her forearm, yet another sported some cherry blossom on her ankle. One of his favorites was a leopard style tattoo which ran all the way up the spine.

One of the highlights in Hertzelberger's memory was an Asian girl, short, with a pleasing smile, almost humble, whose tattoos were delicate roses, which seemed somehow both chaste and submissive, who danced for him so accommodatingly that he kept paying her for yet another dance until he swore he could smell the saline smell of her arousal. He mentioned this to her, impudently, he thought to himself, amazement mingling with pride when she confirmed this, her body riding high above his face so the plastic sequins on her midriff softly scraped his nose.

Hertzelberger sometimes went to Curves on spec and other times he had a specific arrangement to meet a girl. On the former occasions, he would sit at the bar and survey the scene. He would size up all of the girls before making a decision as to which one to approach. Some of the girls would ask him if he wanted a dance but he would politely decline. He would always take his time but would usually know instantaneously when he spotted the one who really turned him on. On the latter, he would relax into one of the comfy chairs on the floor and adopt an insouciant demeanor while waiting for his date.

"Can I sit with you?" A very young, tall, flat-chested girl crouched down alongside Hertzelberger. He immediately knew that she was a beginner. The other girls only ever asked if he wanted a dance.

"Well, if you want, but I'm not buying any dances right now," he said.

"It's okay, babe, just wanted to talk." How Hertzelberger loved the terms of endearment used by the girls: *babe* or *hon* or *sweet* or *cutie*. He had even been called "hot boy," at which point he did wonder if the girl in question was fully in command of all her faculties. Hertzelberger was right. It was the girl's first night and she was nervous. She was a medical student at U. of A., and this was her first foray into the "entertainment" industry. She did not rock his boat, although they ended up having an interesting chat about Obama's healthcare plan. What he did remember about her was the way she handled money. She had folded the notes horizontally and wedged them between her fingers, something she said she had seen the girls in Vegas do.

It was three o'clock in the afternoon one Thursday when Hertzelberger arrived at the club. He had just come from a meeting of his local "Israel at 60" support group, at which his suggestions in relation to a fund-raising event had been unanimously approved. He was in such a good mood that he spontaneously decided to head for his parallel universe on the Oracle Road, rather than return to the office. He calculated that he would have time to draft the contract on Isaac Singer's property acquisition between eight and ten in the morning, before the weekly partners' meeting in the boardroom. In essence, Hertzelberger reckoned, it was all a juggling act, and he was certainly good at keeping a load of balls in the air.

Hertzelberger would always get a buzz the moment he entered the club. He would imbibe that overwhelming smell of perfume which simply reeked of sex. As far as he was concerned, it was an effective aphrodisiac. He invariably buried his nose into the girls' necks and inhaled. "I love your perfume," he would say. "What's it called?" They would tell him, but it would just go in one ear and out the other. Hertzelberger was a past master at flattery. He knew exactly how to make the girls feel good about themselves, even though most of them were bombarded with compliments from morning until night. He would say things like, "You are sheer class, do you know that? You are a work of art, nothing more, nothing less. Your skin is translucent and your teeth are as flawless as the finest pearls."

Some of them could see through him, but the majority liked the sound of what he said and found him genuinely funny.

Hertzelberger liked observing the various techniques of the girls as they worked their way up, down, and around the stage poles, and he regarded himself as an expert by now. A few of his frequent and special rendezvous partners were real pros. Others were decidedly poor—awkward or patently bored by what they were doing. He also liked it very much when they danced for him: the way they rode his lap, the way they draped their hair over his face, the way they placed their nipples on his lips, and the way they placed their lips on his organ and created vibrations.

"What do you call it when you do that?" Hertzelberger had asked one of the girls.

"We call it the lip vibrator," she said seriously.

"Oh, of course, dear, silly question, really."

Hertzelberger was chatting to Dwayne, the daytime restroom attendant, a laid back African American, with a silvery tongue, who had seen it all in his eleven years at the club. Dwayne never tired of telling all and sundry how he had been eating copious amounts of food and pussy since he was in junior high school. By fascinating contrast, the night time restroom attendant was an equally relaxed German guy called Stefan who liked to discuss culture, politics, and philosophy. He was always on the lookout for highbrow clientele who knew stuff about the likes of Goethe, Brecht, Kant, and Wittgenstein.

They were still shooting the breeze when in walked a vision of loveliness that literally took his breath away. Alicia stood well over six feet tall in her heels and Hertelberger, a mere five feet six inches, literally had to crane his neck to see her face. She was so beautiful it was almost painful. Her legs extended upwards a very long way, and her bosom was more than ample. Her skin was a magnificent dark brown color, with an almost imperceptible bronze tint, and her face was mesmerizing. He had never seen such a smile. This girl was an Amazonian goddess, and she had a personality to match. She positively gushed. "So wonderful to meet you, Morris. I love your suit, very classy. We don't get many guys in here dressed like you. You gonna come to the Champagne Room with me, baby. You won't regret it."

It took Hertzelberger all of two seconds to reply in the affirmative.

The set-up at Curves was that if you contracted with a girl to dance for you in the main lounge you paid ten bucks per dance. If you opted for the VIP area, which was partially screened off, it was fifteen. If you went for broke and opted for the Champagne Room, which was designed to accommodate a maximum of five or six couples, it would set you back an entry fee of twenty bucks and another twenty a dance. Naturally, all the girls loved to get customers into the Champagne Room. It took no time at all to rack up a two or three hundred dollar bill in there, and the ones who danced on the pole (some just waitressed and lap danced) really loved it because it meant that they would not be called to pole dance, back-to-back, on the three main stages. The girls gave thirty percent of their takings to the management, which most of them seemed to be happy with.

Hertzelberger would go through periods of infatuation with one girl or another. The one with Alicia was the most intense he had experienced. They had a lot of fun in the Champagne Room, she French kissed him, and they seemed to hit it off. She loved his dry sense of humor and intellect. He recounted his favorite story about the time he and the rabbi's wife had been frolicking, semi-naked, on the rabbi's sofa when the rabbi arrived home. He'd grabbed his shoes and shirt and hidden behind the sofa. He had not been able to leave for almost an hour as the rabbi had plunked himself down on the sofa and not moved. At one point the rabbi dropped his mobile phone, which rolled around the side of the sofa and landed inches from where he was crouching. As the rabbi bent down to recover it, he was so close that Hertzelberger could smell the garlic on his breath.

Hertzelberger really liked the way he and Alicia opened up to each other. "I'm something different," said Alicia. "I go to the gym and stay lean, but most of the girls are spongebobs. They hate that I do better than them. There is a lot of jealousy at this club. I call them haterz, with a z. I keep telling them, 'Why do you keep watching me? If you weren't too busy watching me you'd be making money too.' And I'm the only one who's not permanently wasted on drink and drugs. I don't care. I came here to make money, not friends."

"Don't worry about those second-raters, honey." Hertelberger never lost an opportunity to do a bit of schmoozing. "You are simply the best, in a league of your own."

A few days after their mid-afternoon get-together in the Champagne Room, Hertzelberger received a text from Alicia: "Will be at Raiders Reef on Golf Links for two weeks. Will you come and see me, baby?"

"I would never have schlepped out here to see any of those losers, and I'm sure the same applies to the other Curves regulars. I don't get it," he said ruefully, as they sat at the bar at Raiders Reef, a decidedly second-rate establishment way out in the southeast sector of town. "Why wouldn't the management back you? You must be one of their best earners?"   "Exactly, that's what I told them, but they just wanna punish me. It's vindictive. Such fuckers."

"Poor baby," said Hertzelberger. "My poor little exiled one."

"Just gotta take it up the tail pipe, darling," Alicia said ruefully.

Apparently, she had had a dispute with a customer over money and the bosses had reprimanded her and banished her to Raiders Reef, which they also owned. Hertzelberger naively expected that his loyalty would be rewarded. The opposite happened.

He arranged to meet her at the club one day at three p.m. She turned up in her everyday gear and said that she was going to put her club gear on. Hertzelberger waited patiently at the bar for half an hour. She came back without having done so.

"Listen, babe, I'm not going to get dressed today. It's not worth it. There aren't enough people here. But we can be out of here right now if you want."

"Out of here?" Hertzelberger was confused. It had never been his intention to venture outside the club with any of the girls. Tucson was too small a place. You would usually bump into someone you knew.

"Yes, can you give me six? We'll go to a motel across the street, and I'll show you the time of your life."

"I, I don't know. Six? Do you mean six hundred?"

"I sure as hell don't mean sixty bucks, Morris."

"Listen Alicia, I'm not made of money. I don't think this is such a good idea."   "Alright, five hundred then. I will take four-fifty, and fifty is the cost of the motel. Come on, baby. You won't regret it. We'll snort some of the white stuff."

For a split second he thought she'd said, "the right stuff." Then he realized she'd said "white" and not "right." It was a good thirty years since he had indulged in that sort of thing. As far as he remembered, it had not had the slightest effect on him. But then again he had once consumed thirty Bloody Marys in an hour when he was eighteen and not thrown up or had a headache. All his friends thought he was weird.

"Well, alright then, but we must be discreet, okay?" Even as he found himself relenting he did not feel good about it. Alicia had one or two things to sort out, and she suggested that Hertzelberger wait in the car for her. He realized after fifteen minutes that she wasn't coming. He thought of going back into the club but decided against it. What would it achieve? He would only humiliate himself. He waited another fifteen minutes and then left.

Maybe she did it just to prove she could—to make the point that no customer should ever take her for granted or undervalue her. The next day he sent her a text. "What happened? Did someone offer you six hundred? I think I got you all wrong."

A couple of days later she texted back. "Sorry. I was drunk and had a problem with my ex. He beat me up."

Hertzelberger replied immediately: "Go to police. Still luv ya xxx." The fact she replied, even in the shorthand of the text, pleading violence to herself at the hands of some mustachioed villainous truck driver, as he pictured the man, gave him pleasure. And even though he knew full well that she was a real operator, he just could not bring himself to ditch her. He was well and truly hooked, he said to himself with rueful worship. He just loved her company, her glamour, and, first and foremost, her body.

Nevertheless, as things would have it, he quickly took up with an exotic girl of Filipino and Hawaiian extraction. Her name was Lauren, and she was very laid-back and funny, even if not always intentionally so. He once texted her, "Miss you, baby. Do you miss me?"

And she replied: "Of course, I moss you, my love."

It was Sunday afternoon and Hertzelberger, his wife, Barbara, and teenage daughters, Simone and Michelle, were enjoying their Sunday roast at home.

"Dad, can we go to San Francisco this summer?" inquired the alternative-cultured seventeen-year-old, Simone.

"Certainly, darling, but only if you remove those nose studs. Earrings I can handle, even a little tattoo on your ankle, but not those." As Hertzelberger attempted to influence his daughter's appearance, he was disgusted at his own hypocrisy. He loved practically all of the body art on show at Curves, but maybe it was some kind of latent guilt that made him castigate his daughter for doing the same thing.

"Oh, forget it, Dad. I'm not getting rid of them, period. Just let me be who I am. Christ almighty!" Hertzelberger stayed silent.

"Darling, don't forget we've got the Green girl's bat mitzvah on Sunday afternoon, will you?"

"No, of course not, sweetheart. It's in my di... ar, ar, although, what time is it?" he found himself blurting out as he suddenly remembered that he had a rendezvous with Lulu, the Native American girl at Curves.

"Threeish, I think," said Barbara. "Why, do you have other plans?"

"Yes, I mean no. It's fine. I had planned to go to the gym, but I can go on Saturday instead." He would have to text Lulu to re-schedule.

Hertzelberger had an hour or so to spare one weekday afternoon, so he decided to pop into the club on spec and see who was around. Alicia was usually there in the afternoons. He always kept a clean shirt in the car so that he could swiftly dispense with the perfume-ridden one after he had left. As he got out of the car, he grabbed some legal papers because there was something he needed to check relating to a land deal he was involved in. There was a new guy up front who was very businesslike.

"What are those, sir?"

"Er, what are you referring to?" said Hertzelberger.

"The papers, sir."

"Oh, that's a legal contract. I'm a lawyer," said Hertzelberger, somewhat taken aback.

"I'm not sure if you can bring those in, sir. They're very strict here."

"It's not a gun, my friend. It's paper, for God's sake."

"Rules are rules, sir."

"Well, of course they are, young man. But under what possible rule might it be not allowed for me to bring a private legal contract relating to one of my client's property purchases into a strip club with me?"

"I have no idea, sir, but I must check it with my manager."

The manager had no problem with the papers.

"Sorry about that, sir. The young man is under strict instructions not to allow anyone to bring anything into the club. Back in the day, there was an incident when a customer brought in a laptop which was then used as a weapon, so the management has been very touchy since then."

"Don't worry about me," said Hertzelberger, jovially, "The worst I can do with this contract is to turn it into some weird origami object to impress one of the girls."

The managers at Curves were usually big guys and walked up and down with clipboards. They would check on the girls, particularly on the amount of dances they were giving to their clients, and would stamp the hands and take the twenty bucks from all the customers who had been lured into the Champagne Room.

Lo and behold, he ran into Alicia, who was not a happy bunny. "It's so bad here today. I mean, look at it, it's dead. I was just about to go, actually."

"Oh, well, how about I book you for six dances right off the bat? That's sixty bucks. And you won't have to do all of them, baby. Two or three and I'll be plenty excited."

"You know me, honey, no staying power." Alicia usually made between three and four grand a week, and she did not like it at all when things were slow.

"Why not go to LA or Vegas?" asked Hertzelberger. "Wouldn't that be more lucrative?"

"Oh, yeah, I could earn like a grand a day there, but I'm into Tucson right now. Slower pace, more laid-back, and all that. And I can live very well here. Actually, I just rented a big loft space downtown."

"Good for you, girl." Hertzelberger had to hand it to her. She was dynamic, confident, and knew exactly what she wanted. When Hertzelberger asked her what the managers with the clipboards were like, she replied: "They feel powerful and intimidate quite a few of the girls. But not me. I intimidate them."

Hertzelberger watched spellbound as Alicia rode the pole on the main stage. And he was not the only one. At least eight other guys were savoring her every move. No less accomplished than any ballet or flamenco dancer he'd ever seen, she was the consummate professional. She'd shown him all the moves: the crucifix-serpent, the flatline scorpio, the reverse roll double hook dismount, and the chopper climb, all of which struck Hertzelberger as fiendishly difficult but which Alicia could do with her eyes closed. The contrast with the lame way some of the girls performed on stage could not have been starker—walking in metronomic fashion around the pole, flopping down onto their bellies like beached whales, and clacking their heels together appeared to be the full extent of their repertoire—it was like comparing a Glenlivit to a bottle of Moonshine.

Michelle ran up to Hertzelberger before he'd even had a chance to take his jacket off and drop his umbrella into the stand. She pecked him on the neck, on the very same spot Alicia had nibbled at an hour or so earlier. "You smell nice, Daddy. Are you wearing cologne?"

"Yes, my angel, it's my new Givenchy Pour Homme. Glad you like it." He would always spray a little bit on himself after leaving Curves so as to mask the smell of perfume or, at the very least, to confuse the issue should the subject ever arise.

"Morris, is that you?" Barbara called out from the kitchen, where she and Lily, her long-serving Mexican home help were busy preparing the Shabbat dinner.

"Hi, honey. Got you your favorite truffle balls from The Chocolate Depot."

"Gold star shmoochy poochy. Big helping of egg and onion for you tonight."

"Too funny. You two are priceless." Michelle doubled up as she laughed out loud, her fine, raven black hair cascading over her head as she did so. Hertzelberger observed his daughter's pale 16-year old neck, so pure and free of any worldly imperfections. He had become a past-master at rolling his knuckles up and down the sweaty necks of lap dancers and gently kneading into the pressure points on the backs of their heads with his stubby thumbs.

Hertzelberger always made sure that he accumulated a few brownie points with Barbara when he knew that, further down the line, he'd likely be dropping a minor bombshell. As they tucked into their gefilte fish and borscht, he looked over at his wife of twenty-four and a half years. She really didn't look much different than the day they first met, while riding the escalator at Macy's in San Francisco. She still had the same sweet smile, the same chiseled nose, the same magnified lenses, the same floppy ears.

"Guess what, sweetheart, a client can't make it to *West Side Story* at the Tucson Music Hall so we got the tickets."

"Oh, Morris, what a good boy you are. I may spoil you and wear my new fluffy, chiffon nightgown tonight."

"Ooh, very sexy, Mom," said Michelle. "You kept that quiet."

Then Simone chimed in, "Watch out, Mom. Dad wants something. First the truffles, now the tickets."

"Nonsense, Simone. I've always loved to spoil your mom. Quite the cynic, our eldest."

"Dad's right, darling. You really shouldn't always be looking to find the bad in people."

"Whatever," said Simone in that utterly defiant seventeen-year-old kind of way.

Hertzelberger was always up for evening concerts at the music hall because it was only stone's throw from his office at Tucson's downtown La Placita Village, a funky, fountain laden, multi-colored office and restaurant complex. He knew of no other place remotely like it. Resplendent with a whole host of bright hues, orange, red, pink, mauve, green, and turquoise, he loved its fluid configuration and the solidity of its adobe walls. Ambling through its shady walkways and drinking coffee in its peaceful, *mercado* style courtyard helped his thought process.

As Hertzelberger and Alicia sipped cocktails by the bamboo pool at Miami's art deco Catalina Hotel and Beach Club, he reflected on how well he'd handled the subject of his trip with Barbara. Right after telling her that all of the directors were due a twenty thousand end of year bonus, he mentioned matter-of-factly that he would have to accompany a client to Miami to tie up an important land deal. If he performed well, there was another mega deal in the offing in New Mexico. Barbara hadn't batted an eyelid. She had even asked him if she should buy him some new shirts from Benetton.

Hertzelberger's bald pate popped gently out of the shimmering water like a brown boiled egg bobbing up in the pan. He rested it on his tanned arms and was enjoying the feeling of the hot concrete underneath them when he heard a deep, lilting voice.

"Hey mister, you awake?"

Sounds Appalachian, thought Hertzelberger, who had fallen into the most pleasant of reveries.

"Hey, mister, I know you. You're that bigshot lawyer out of Tucson, who fucked me over on a land deal, remember, the lot on 22nd and Pantano?"

Only then did he realize that it was he who was being addressed. He looked up and saw a tall man wearing Ray-Bans and a pair of yellow and green psychedelic swimming trunks. Hertzelberger felt a nasty pang in his stomach, and he tried to act dumb.

"Er, you sure, buddy? I think you got the wrong guy."

"Come on, dude, that's lame. You gotta be able to do better than that. Let me remind you. You were doing all the dirty work for that rotten Republican congressman, what was his name? Oh, yes, Ward Underwood. Turns out he was able to offer thirty grand over the odds 'cos he illegally used his re-election campaign contributions. And you vouched for the guy's integrity. Said you'd represented him for twelve years and were sure he was clean. That help you remember?"

"Okay, what do you want from me?" Hertzelberger asked the man, who, unsurprisingly, was looking rather smug.

"Funny thing. I always had a feeling I'd have a chance to get even with you. What is it they say? What goes around comes around. Yeh, that's it." The man laughed heartily, a rather cartoonish "he he he" sort of laugh. "I'd guess you're a married man with kids, and here you are hanging in Miami with a very hot black babe. Wow, gotta hand it to you, you are one smooth operator."

This time, his laugh was even more pronounced and attracted the interest of one or two folks poolside. Luckily, Alicia was up in the room having a rest. "So what do you want?" said Hertzelberger again.

"Dunno yet, but I'll let you know when I think of something. Don't disappear now, 'cos then I really will get mad and come after you." The man turned on his heel and walked off without glancing back at Hertzelberger.

"What's wrong, Mo? You've hardly said a word all night," said Alicia as she stirred her blue curacao flavored Margherita.

"It's alright, love, just a little bump in the road, nothing the Hertzanator can't handle."

"If you say so, hon, but remember, two heads are better than one. And you know what a sharp cookie I am. They don't call me 'A-Force Alicia' for nothing, you know."

"I know, I know. It's always reassuring to have you on my side, my sweet." Alicia slid her hand over Hertzelberger's groin and blew gently into his ear.

Hertzelberger angsted all night. Tossing and turning, his mind racing, he fluctuated between figuring out a way to mollify the man and lamenting the reality of his deceit. He knew that he was a man with a conscience and a deep love for his wife and children. But he had his dark side, and there was no point fighting it. It was in his DNA. Humans were all, at the basest of levels, simians. One thing he was certain of was that he would never let an opportunist like the poolside revenge seeker anywhere near his family. He would act decisively to prevent such a thing from happening. Hertzelberger had never owned a gun but now might be the time to acquire one. As he drifted in and out of a sweaty sleep, a horrible image of the man, stone-eyed, slumped against a bathtub and surrounded by blood, kept on reappearing.

And then it came to him, delivered on a silver platter from on high. The perfect solution. He would sell the guy the lot he owned in the Armory Park subdivision. He could have it dirt cheap. To tell the truth, it had been years since Hertzelberger had even thought about it. Underwood himself had sold it to him for a song so he'd still make a profit. It was one of those messy parcels that needed to be worked on painstakingly, a slow-burner, and he had neither the time nor the inclination to give it the attention it required. He could picture the silvery-tongued slimeball sweet talking all the tenants, not to mention the bureaucrats in the City of Tucson Planning Department.

"Thought I'd find you in here, you dirty dawg."

"Hey, Brent. Take a seat and tell me what havoc you've been creating down there in Armory Park?" Hertzelberger was so much happier now that the big Virginian was on his side.

"You know how it is, Morris. There's a lot of cultivating and lubricating to be done. But I can do that shit. Years of practice."

"I don't doubt it for a minute, Brent. You can certainly talk the ass off a brown monkey."

"Gee, thanks, Morris. Coming from you, I take that as a compliment."

"Oh it is, Brent. It is. Now, which of these beauties do you fancy a jabber with?"

Hertzelberger was having yet another bad night. As Barbara snored royally at his side, her face open and trusting in sleep, in the gloomy half-light the yellow sponge earplugs looked like the tiny buds of horns on a young lamb. Now he was wide awake and sweating profusely. For about a week, he'd been enduring a particularly bad bout of insomnia accompanied by burning hot flushes in his legs. It was all a consequence of the overwhelming guilt he'd been feeling since returning from the mini-break in Miami with Alicia. Guilt brought about by his continual deceit. For sure, in years gone by he'd had introspective moments when he questioned his moral worth, and the answers that emerged ranged from, at worst, disgust to, at best, a "no one's perfect" shrug of the shoulders. The idea that the good he did would always outweigh the bad had always been prevalent.

Now, however, Hertzelberger was in the grip of a much more thoroughgoing existential crisis and it frightened him. Never before had such a potent cocktail of fear and self-loathing afflicted him. The Miami trip was the first time he'd ever travelled with a mistress, so it certainly represented a departure from past practice. And the encounter with Brent Mickelson hadn't helped. Yes, he'd adroitly averted danger and always put on an act in front of Brent, but the truth was the whole episode had left him emotionally drained. He did not look back on the Ward Underwood episode with pride, and it prompted him to reflect on what other skeletons might be lurking in the shadows. The feelings of disgust and self-loathing were most uncomfortable, but at least he could understand where they were coming from. He'd invariably been perceived by society as being of the utmost decency and moral rectitude. But when he began to really examine inside his soul he saw that he was nothing of the sort. A self-serving, arrogant narcissist was a much more accurate assessment of who he was.

Hertzelberger had always been a devout Jew and knew full well that the Jewish God was a tough taskmaster who could be extremely vengeful. It may have been because he'd reached a certain age and had seen one or two friends pass away, but, increasingly, he'd been dwelling on the journey he would be making from this world to the "world to come" as the Jews called it. The key element was the state of a man's soul and the amount of divine radiance it would be able to absorb in the world to come. Good deeds in this world would ensure that the soul would be in good shape to receive God's benevolence. Hertzelberger was becoming ever more preoccupied by the state of decay he believed his soul to be in. He'd had one particularly terrible nightmare about being present in the city of Sodom and Gomorrah when God "rained down burning sulfur" on its unclean, fornicating inhabitants.

As time went by, Hertzelberger managed to pull himself back from the abyss. He endeavored to nourish his soul and build up capital in the imaginary Bank of Good Deeds. He offered his time more readily to the temple and engaged more actively in philanthropy. The libido thing was still there, though, always loitering with intent, in the shadows. If he could only remain in the black, Hertzelberger told himself, all would be well. He was, more and more, yes—absolutely!—convinced of it.

Things Happen In Threes

It's eight a.m. on a cold, overcast Saturday morning in December. Me and the boys have just had one of our mammoth movie and backgammon nights, and I haven't been to bed. I shuffle out to the mailbox and, as I look down, notice that my Wildcats T has got the mother of all reefer holes smack in the middle of the chest, not to mention the orangey-brown remnants of my chicken tikka masala. "You slob, Ayles," I say to myself, "once a reprobate, always a reprobate I guess," and I giggle maniacally in that familiar "still drunk in the morning" kind of way.

The snowy tips of the Tucson Mountains loom large above the thick swirl of black and gray nimbus clouds. The moist atmosphere suggests that the bloated sky will soon yield up the precipitation that the Sonoran desert so craves. An eerie stillness fills the air. I can feel the rivulets of damp sweat running down the nape of my neck and working their way through the flimsy clusters of hair that line the top of my back.

I clumsily yank open the mailbox and the usual jetsam burst forth. Same old crap: junk mail from Direct TV, Terminix, and Geico, begging letters from the liberal do-gooders brigade—Amnesty, Greenpeace, Care International, et al. If they only took the trouble to call me once I could tell them that I'm a narcissistic, gun-toting, property developer, whose only concerns are me, my alter-ego, and my wallet. How many trees do they waste on me every year—goddamn bills from Cox, Southwest Gas, Verizon, and so forth plus a postcard from my folks, who are taking a vacation in Louisiana, Louisi-fuckin-ana. Hanging out probably right now in some alligator bayou, maxing out on Zydeco and chili burgers. I feel sorry for them—and for anybody who isn't like me. But they're probably as happy as pigs in shit, so good, Mom and Dad, I say.

A purple letter slips out from the sheaf of crap. Handwritten, no less! I flip it over and see the name of my old flame, Lorna Sergeant, which calls back memories immediately—good fuck now and then—loud yelling usually. I hear a high-pitched foreign voice.

"Yes. Good morning, sir. You need handyman? I fix it up everything in house, inside outside. My service value added, okay. You wanna give me try out?"

I'm a moody arrogant shit and would normally have sent a guy like this on his way without a second glance, but it just so happens that my man threw his back out and I need a replacement. I look up. A runt with closely cropped white hair and cauliflower ears is beaming up at me. He's wearing overalls which have funky tape measure shoulder straps. Admittedly reluctant to indulge the runt I nonetheless find myself saying, "Well, mister, you just might be in luck." I pause momentarily before saying sternly, "But listen up. You know what you're doing, right? I don't like having my time wasted." I have a bit of trouble keeping up the severity of my stare at him because he's looking back at me with that kind of cheerful optimism that, from sheer persistence, is like a toe in the door. So I set my stare past him as if figuring out the long odds of getting hit by a truck the next minute—that way I manage to look both tough and resigned at the same time.

"I serious, man. No time to waste. If I don't buy my mother super dress for her fifty-year wedding, she, you know...." He slides a grimy index finger across his neck. I notice there's a really weird bump on its right side that looks like a piece of pastry with a shrunken cherry on top. I look at it fractionally longer than I should and, again, though I know better, for some reason, let myself be suckered.

"Ok, I'll give you a shot, but I gotta warn you, amigo, you jerk me around and I'll make your life...hell....Understand?"

"Yes, sir, but before you bust ball let me to send that damn dress to mother. I more scared of her than you."

I'm supposed to laugh, but I give the runt a little pained smile.

I own a lot out on Houghton and Valencia which has three forty-foot steel containers on it, and I need to get rid of them a.s.a.p. I decide to give Vlad, the grinning Georgian, as I call him, the job. He can do whatever he wants with the things. I just want them to disappear.

Vlad left the Soviet Union in 1983, arriving in New York with his birth certificate, toothbrush, Bible, pack of playing cards, spirit-level, blanket, Dinamo Tiblisi soccer club pendant, and seven bucks.

"I follow American Dream," he often says. "America gave me bread, I no kid you. In our town many times there is no food in shelves in shops. We could stand in line many hours for food. I lie down hungry too many times. You know, if no bread in house, I feel, you know, bad. Even I have one dozen pork chops and twelve-pack of buds. I must to have bread. When I tear that bread open and eat it fresh and warm it is best feeling in world.

Vlad slept pretty rough for a while but then found work in construction. The Russian pirates who hired him paid him a buck twenty an hour and with great kindness gave him a mattress on a damp, concrete basement floor in a six-to-a-room house in the Bronx.

"You know, I always can make laugh about things when I remember time I was in prison in Tibilisi. Then I had bed, only three in cell, had toilet, had heater, and no cockroach like in Bronx. And no super loud rapper music all night. But still...in U.S.A. I am free. Nobody listen my phone, no one follow me, no one threaten me to go to gulag in Siberia," he says, looking sad, pissed off and happy all at once.

I never fully get a grip on why Vlad did a six-month stint in jail, but it was something to do with illegal possession of Western videos. He's a big John Wayne fan, I know that much. Once he scared the hell out of me by creeping up on me as I was lying, half asleep, on the couch. I felt a cold gun on my temple and a voice was saying, "Okay, stick zem up, Big Chief Sitting Bullshit or I blow out brains." I wasn't happy about this. According to Vlad the gun was a replica of the one Wayne used in the movie *Stagecoach*. He told me he bought it for three dollars in a New York thrift shop.

Lorna and I had been pretty tight during our time together at Sunnyside High. We played hooky a lot and hung out at the Bone Yard near the air force base or at Magic Carpet miniature golf on Speedway. We'd usually pop a few E's, which ensured our experiences were very mellow. I'll never forget the huge sculptures at the Magic Carpet, especially the T-Rex, the monkey, and the Tiki head. Being on top of the Tiki head gave us a good buzz, but when I think about it now I can't believe we took such a risk. It wouldn't have taken much to flip over that flimsy circular railing. And as for the bone yard, it was like being in another world. All those airplane carcasses, which looked to us like whales with their mouths open. We'd act out scenarios where we flew to other planets and fought with fire-breathing, reptilian-like dwarves and millions of fanged, poisonous bats. One time, Lorna got carried away and stabbed me in the leg with a sharp stick. I needed fifteen stitches and, to this day, have a neat four-inch scar on my thigh.

How it happened was kind of odd. I mean, it wasn't as though we'd been lusting after each other. Sure, we were adolescents, in the process of discovering our sexuality, but we were best friends and had not seen each other as potential sex partners. One day, we were messing around at Lorna's folks' house, while they were out of town. I remember she was wearing a tight-fitting, pink, turtleneck sweater through which I could see her bra, a sexy lace number. All of a sudden I felt horny and I said, "Hey, nice bra. Is it from Victoria Secret?"

She laughed. "It is, actually. Wow, you're observant—I'm impressed."

"Can I have a closer look?" I asked. In a heartbeat we were French kissing, and I had unhooked the bra and was fondling her firm, pear-shaped breasts. We lay there on our backs, smoking and wondering how it had happened. The sex wasn't great. It didn't feel natural and was all over in a flash. But the issue was whether it would just be a one-timer or whether we would really get it on. We never satisfactorily resolved that question. We continued sleeping together, albeit infrequently, and we certainly had some feelings for each other. But I would not say that we were ever emotionally involved, and I would never have described us as soul mates. For a start, she considered me to be too uptight, and I regarded her as too demanding. Once, several years later, when I had just started wheeling and dealing in property, she wanted me to take her to Phoenix for the weekend to see the Cardinals play and go to a Springsteen gig. I would've been all over it but had to stick around in Tucson because I had an issue with a squatter.

"Get Bobby to do it," she said.

Like Bobby had the faintest idea how to evict someone. The only thing Bobby was good for was disposing of shit: mud, concrete, asbestos, sewage pipes, dead coyotes. You name it, he could make it disappear. "No Lorne, I'm the only one who can handle it. Trust me, evictions can get messy."

"Whatever you say, Danny boy, but I'll tell you one thing. You gotta ease up one of these days. Too much good stuff's passing you by."

"Apart from our extra-vehicular activity," I shot back. "I'm always up for that, right honey?" I was referring to our proclivity for fucking in the back of my Buick at various locations around town, at any time of the day or night. The most daring place we did it was in the parking lot of the Tucson Convention Center during a concert. We were both high and in full aphrodisiac-enhanced mode. Funny, really, because I wasn't adventurous in anything else I did.

We'd carried on our strange, category-defying relationship for around six years, when Lorna was transferred by Cricket, the phone company for whom she was a sales rep, to Vegas. We kept in touch for a while, and she told me that she'd hooked up with a hot-shot banker who had a sideline selling stuffed elk and deer heads on e-bay. We hadn't communicated for at least five years when I received her letter, the very same day on which I first met Vlad. Because I firmly believed that things really did happen in threes, I wondered what the third interesting event of that particular day would turn out to be. When I was eleven, I broke my arm, stole something from a shop, and kissed a girl, all for the first time and all on the same day.

Lorna's letter isn't an easy read. She's broken up with the banker—he cheated on her—had a miscarriage, and found out that her mother had been diagnosed with lung cancer. She's planning to move back to Tucson and is asking if she could stay with me or at one of my properties until she gets back on her feet. She's depressed and her work has given her as much time off as she needs, but only four weeks of it will be paid. Acts of generosity are very rare in my world. When I was fourteen, I helped an old lady who I'd seen trip just a few feet away from me. She was pretty shaken up, so I comforted her and stayed with her for half an hour, even though it meant I missed the start of a football game. The only other good deed I remember doing was about five years ago, when I was in my late twenties. I took a box full of children's toys that I'd found in the basement of a house I was renovating to a thrift shop. I don't normally bother to do that sort of thing, and I'm still not sure why I did it that one time. It might have been something to do with the fact that I recalled there was a thrift shop a minute or so away from the titty bar I was just about to go to.

It's against my better judgment, and I have a bad feeling about the whole thing. People always counsel against taking in friends in need, but, nonetheless, I decide to help Lorna out. We were very close, and I'd feel guilty if I reject her in her hour of need. Well, let me qualify that a little. When I say I would feel guilty I think that's somewhat of an exaggeration since I think it would take a helluva lot more than that for me to be affected by an emotion as strong as guilt. Let's just say that it may cause me to question whether I'm being unfair to her.

For the first week or so, Lorna crashes at my place, which is fine, but I'm soon craving my own company. I move her into a house down south, at 6th Ave and 36th Street, a quintessential Tucson location, where two Mexican restaurants keep company with a tire shop, Hispanic Alcoholics Anonymous, a Salvation Army branch, a feed store, a funeral parlor, and a factory converted into a Latino church. For me, this is Tucson's urban eco-system writ large, a perfect example of Anglo-Latino cross-pollination. The fact that quite a few of the street names in the residential areas of predominantly Hispanic South Central Tucson—Lincoln Street, MacArthur Street, Illinois Street, Ohio Street, Rodeo Drive—are closer to mainstream American heritage, while a lot of those in equivalent neighborhoods elsewhere in the city—Placita Estrellita, Vereda Felicidad, Calle del Suerte, Arroyo Chico—suggest the Latino influence, is a perfect indication of that fact.

We have just eaten an excellent lunch at the modest Pico de Gallo Tacqueria, its yellow exterior wall adorned with a painted cartoon rooster and red and blue lettering. A single neon sign is its only concession to modernity. As we stand outside, the luminous light reflects the branches of a mesquite tree onto a low-slung yellow wall across the street. The atmosphere is languorous, the calm punctuated periodically by the odd pick-up, chock full of assorted detritus. In the distance, we can see the shimmering, watery heat rising off the tarmac.

Lorna is vulnerable and I can sense that she would like a little bit more than just a shoulder to lean on. But I really don't want to go there. One of my golden rules is never to go back. Nothing is ever the same second time around is what I believe. My friends think I'm crazy, but I never even watch the same movie twice. One guy I know has seen Blade Runner sixty times. He's a nut job in my book. We reminisce about old times, and she reminds me about how we used to run through the Manson tunnels carrying stolen police flares and how we'd surf the rapids on the Rillito Wash at Craycroft and River during the monsoon season. We'd make a doughnut-style dinghy out of the inner tube of a car tire and tie it with a polypropylene rope to one of the bridge pillars. "We must have been mad to do all that shit. Wasn't it dangerous?" I say.

"Of course it was, but we were young and carefree. Oh, what I'd give to turn the clock back." Lorna's lost in her own thoughts.

All I know is that I never hanker after the past. What's gone is gone. I wouldn't change anything. I've always liked the song "Je ne regrette rien." That will definitely be my epitaph.

I must admit, I do like having Lorna around. We enjoy each other's company and there's nothing we can't talk about. We have complete trust in each other and value each other's opinions, which are never sugar-coated. Too many people I know walk around in a delusional state because those around them don't tell them the truth. She tells me straight out that my personal grooming is not what it should be: apparently my eyebrows needed trimming as did my nasal hair.

About two months after Lorna's arrival in Tucson, I get a call from Vlad, who knows her because he's been over to the house to fix a leak in the bathroom. "Er, boss. Sorry disturbing you but we got small problem down here at Lorna's house. There is one javelina around here. He kill neighbor's small poodle dog and neighbor go crazy. He blame Lorna. He say she feeds javelinas, and then they come back every day, very aggressive, and if they don't get food they are yelling all night and ripping up everything. He say they smash his gate. He is going to report you to council. He say there is fine for feeding animals. He is crazy, this guy. He punch fence. I think he maybe break his own hand."

"What the fuck? You gotta be kidding me. Jesus fucking Christ. Please tell me I'm having a bad dream. Feeding javelinas. What is *wrong* with that girl?" There's no way I'm going down there now. I'm stoned and I've got company. "Look, just sort it out between you. Tell the guy to calm down. I'll come and speak with him tomorrow. Get his name and number and I'll call him in the morning, okay?"

"Okay, boss, we will deal with situation now, don't worry."

I meet with the guy the next day and try to placate him by agreeing to pay for the damage and buy him a new dog. He's very pissed off. Wants to know why he shouldn't report me. And how are we going to sort out the javelina problem? They're bound to be back. Fortunately, I know my shit on this subject. We buy two big squirt guns, one for him and one for us, and fill them with one part ammonia and nine parts water. They definitely don't like being sprayed with that stuff. Then we fill two aluminum cans with pebbles and wrap them in foil. They are normally scared off by a combination of the noise and the flash. Plan B, which is very much a last resort, is to erect single-strand electric fencing eight to ten inches above the ground. I tell him to wipe down all his trash bins with bleach, and he might as well spray some of the ammonia solution on the trash bags themselves. He appreciates my hands-on approach, and I manage to appease him. But he expects me to keep an eye on my tenants and make sure they don't do such stupid things again.

One thing that occurs to me later is that it was 9 o'clock in the evening when Vlad called me. Why would he be there at night?

"So how come you called me and not Lorna? And what were you doing there at that time anyway?" I ask him when I next see him.

He immediately looks sheepish. "I was over there fixing up something for her. Just for favor, boss."

And then the penny dropped. "You dirty dog, Vlad. You've been doing some plumbing over there, but not the type I thought you were doing."

He's squirming. "Please, boss. You not tell my wife. She kill me."

"No, I won't tell your wife. I don't rat on people—it's not my style. But next time you decide to fuck a friend of mine perhaps you could ask me first, you fucking jerk." I make out I'm angrier than I really am. Sometimes, you just gotta flex your muscles.

"Very sorry, boss. You right. Won't happen this again. Sorry. Sorry."

"Why didn't you tell me Vlad was dicking you, Lorne?"

"I know I should have mentioned it. I guess I was embarrassed. Didn't expect to be making out with a middle-aged foreigner with a very thick accent. Anyway, we only did it twice and that's the end of it. I'm sorry, Daniel, I really am. And about the javelinas, too."

"You worry me sometimes, Lorne. You sure you're okay? We don't want any more dramas, do we?"

"I'm doing good. Don't worry about me. I just mess up big-time every now and again.

"Just make sure you communicate with me about shit. That way we cover all our bases."

She nods at me and smiles goofily. Crazy broad.

Predictably, Lorna's presence in Tucson has already caused me some irritation. I start to worry about what might be next. From now on I'll need to keep a close eye on those two. At the back of my mind a seed of suspicion has been planted. Individually, they're as good as gold. But together, that's another matter. You just never know how the chemistry between people will impact them. After all, if the javelina incident had never happened, I may never have found out about their little dalliance. True, that wouldn't have been the end of the world, but I'm the kind of person who doesn't like secrets, especially not when they're so close to home. I like to think I know what people in Ayles's world are up to. But, of course, that's totally down to me being a control freak. "Ease up, Ayles. Live your life and let others live theirs, you nosey son of a bitch," I often chastise myself, but letting stuff go is something I'm just not good at.

Oh, I almost forgot. The third thing that happened on the day I met Vlad and received Lorna's letter took place at precisely six minutes before midnight. I'd been surfing the channels and was in the middle of watching a Jim Click ad—I swear that guy could sell a Mazda to a Martian. And who the hell plucks a figure of $5,888 out of the air?—when my front door bell rings. "What the fuck?" I say out loud. I have no clue who that could be. The Jehovah Witnesses aren't due for at least nine hours. Maybe it's my buddy, Al, looking to score some weed. He's the only dude I know who's capable of showing up unannounced at any time of the day or night. I open the door and standing in front of me is a tall, pregnant girl with an anorexic complexion, who's wearing those ubiquitous pink pants with the word "PINK" printed in large black letters just below the waist-line.

She places the palms of her hands on the bump and says, "This is your son, Daniel Ayles."

I'm lost for words but immediately understand that this is a real and, for me, potentially ugly situation. I gesture for her to come in.

"I told you to use a condom, but you so didn't give a shit. Only one time. Long odds, you said."

I look at her but still I can find no words.

"You don't even know who I am, do you? Fucking asshole."

And then I do remember. A Motel 6 in Las Cruces on the way back from a property auction in Albuquerque. She had legs to die for and was all over me. She says she's nineteen weeks and is having the baby. It took her a while to track me down, but she knows she did the right thing. What do I want to do about it?

I can't think straight. I need time. This new scenario has thrown my cozy, ordered universe into turmoil. The words "responsibility" and "fatherhood" are hurtling around my brain. "Shit, shit, shit. What have you done, Ayles?" is the only sentence I can put together in my spinning head. Then my cell phone rings. Lorna's calling. I don't answer it. I rest my head on the sofa, close my eyes, and wish I could wind the clock back to the days when I was still a young buck with less of an ego and without my arrogant sense of untouchability.

Tomboy Border Rat

Jen Williamson and Mario Jesus Romeo de Santa Anna were sitting on the grass of the El Rio neighborhood center at Speedway and Riverview, a stone's throw away from their liquor store. Jen loved hanging out at the El Rio because it was full of wonderful murals by her favorite artist, David Tineo, the iconic Chicano muralist whose work graced many locations in Tucson. Her favorite mural was the one facing Speedway Boulevard, which was full of his usual mixture of La Raza and Mesoamerican iconography. Containing a mass of sumptuous blue sky, on its right side was one of the pyramids at Tenochtitlan. Above it, a Promethean deity gave a ball of the tyrannical fire of the Gods to a worker whose disproportionately long arm and huge fist extended upwards in a gesture of powerful defiance. In the center, a flying eagle held a snake in its claws. According to myth, where an eagle landed on a cactus was where the Aztec would settle.

As they downed a six-pack of Dos Equis, Jen reminisced about her granny who used to regale her with stories of Prohibition-era Arizona: the bent cop who would call in every week at the local speakeasy, behind the hairdresser shop, to collect his envelope; the folks who went blind or were paralyzed after drinking moonshine which contained creosote or lead; how her favorite Prohibition-era cocktail had been "The French 75," named after a World War I artillery piece; how on the day Prohibition was abolished, December 5th 1933, everyone had a street party and walked around with banners which read "Good Old Days Are Back Again."

"You know, I got to thinking the other day Prohibition was such a fucked up social experiment, it reminds me of the immigration prohibition today, equally fucked up and nonsensical. Trouble is, I don't think they'll ever come to their senses like they did with Prohibition," said Jen.

Mario agreed. "No chance Jen Jen. Too much money washing around. All those enforcement folks, you know, the private prison guys, they're the new prohibition profiteers."

Jen, also known as the Tomboy Border Rat, was as hard as nails. She could mix it up with the best of them, and then some. A brazen bigmouth she may have been, but you wrote her off at your peril, as a bunch of folks in the southern Arizona border region had found out at their cost. Her tongue was as acerbic as a spoonful of vinegar, and her left hook connected with the force of a jackhammer breaking into asphalt. One time, in some dive bar or other in Benson, Arizona, Jen ran into a couple of hoary old cowboys, whose machismo was still blinding them to the reality that their sex appeal had gone west with all the indecent haste of a fly-by-night suitcase rancher. They'd watched her sashay suggestively around the pool table before challenging her to a game.   "So missy, you gonna show us what you got?" said the tall one with the scimitar-shaped scar under his right eye. His sidekick, who had a tattoo of a machine gun on his right shoulder, cupped his hands and held them in front of his chest. "We know what she got Bud." They laughed coarsely and high-fived each other. "Rack'em up," said Jen with a straight face. "We're about to find out who's got *cojones* around here. And I'd be surprised if it was you two washed up losers. " Two or three folks at the bar began giggling. The shorter one emitted a guttural noise and made a move towards Jen but his friend put a long arm across him. "Easy Jack. Save your energy for serious shit."

"Fifty bucks a game. Five games minimum," said Jen, slapping a fifty down on the table. An hour later and two hundred fifty greenbacks better off, Jen offered the cowboy a get out of jail card. "Tell you what. I'll give you a chance to win the whole two fifty back. You down a pint of beer quicker than me and it's all yours. You lose and you're outta here." Jen was already ordering another pint before the guy was through his. Neither of them were ever seen in Benson again.

Jen came from conservative, God-fearing, rancher stock. She was born and raised in Benson, a border town with a colorful history which began in 1880 because it had been chosen as the location where the Mexican and American sections of the new Southern Pacific Railroad would be linked. Her earliest memory was being taught by her father to lasso a cow. She'd spend hours and hours practicing on a bale of hay with a stick wedged in it. To this day, she could hear him drumming the technique into her. "Relax your wrist, girl, and start swinging that rope, real slow, left to right. Think of it as a wheel rotating horizontal over your head. Now swing that arm forward, extend it out, and bring your wrist down to shoulder level. That's it, girl. Let that palm open now, swing that loop hard." She learnt that before she learnt to ride a bicycle and before she learnt to read and write for that matter.

Jen's great-grandfather, Walt Williamson, was sheriff of Benson in the late 1880s, as the new town grew exponentially. The railroad attracted thousands of workers and wherever there was labor there was prostitution, gambling, and liquor. So lawless was Arizona at that time that President Chester. A. Arthur threatened to impose martial law there. As for Walt, himself, he was a violent drunkard, who was never more than a cat's whisker away from spectacular implosion.

On a murderously hot night in July 1899, he was involved in a brawl with his own brother in the main street in Benson. A raucous crowd of locals egged the protagonists on. After all, it wasn't often that hothead sheriffs engaged their own siblings in a potentially fatal fight, and in public. Apparently, the bone of contention was their own mother's will, which favored one of them over the other. Walt stabbed his brother in the thigh with a kitchen knife, and the brother bit off half of Walt's ear. After Walt had passed on, the townsfolk erected a plaque to commemorate the event. It read:

On this spot on 11th July, 1899, the Sheriff of Benson, Walt Williamson, with an eight inch knife, did carve into his brother, Joey's thigh. Prostrate on the ground did the victim lie. But, fearing for his life and encouraged by his wife, brave Joey rose and bit off a portion of Walt's ear. And the crowd let out a huge cheer. The flesh and blood of the Williamson family seeped into the Benson soil. To us, they will always be royal.

Right from the get-go Jen was the black sheep of the family. It appeared that she'd inherited Walt's rogue genes. As stubborn a baby as any of her family had ever witnessed—she would shout the house down whenever a nipple was thrust towards her lips and seemed to have some kind of pathological dislike of anything furry. From the age of eight she began brawling with her peers, sniffing glue, and shoplifting. She was described by a Benson policeman as "proper feral." As a teenager, along with the marijuana staple, Jen experimented with peyote and magic mushrooms. Perversely, Jen always maintained that mind-altering drugs were the making of her. "When those chemicals cross my blood-brain barrier I move into a transcendent zone which enables me to see everything so goddam clearly, it's like I got 3-D goggles on. You know, there's an extra dimension open to me, and those choices we all gotta make suddenly seem a whole lot clearer."

As she entered her twenties, one thing became clearer to her than anything else: she had no interest in ranching. She could ride horses and milk cows with her eyes shut, and she liked being out in nature well enough, but it just didn't excite her. There was more to life, there just had to be. When she got up in the morning the last thing she wanted was to know exactly what was going to happen over the course of the next fifteen hours. It was the uncertainty and unpredictability of the urban life that turned her on.

The fact that she showed little or no interest in the life of a rancher pained her father no end. "Shame on you, girl," he would say to her. "Turning your back on a tradition that your forebears built up over generations, well, that's plain wicked."

"I'm sorry, Daddy. I never set out to cause you grief. It's just not in me in the same way it's in you. But I promise to try and make you proud of me whatever I end up doing." She was always conciliatory towards him but could never do the right thing. As if her rejection of the outdoor life wasn't enough, her liberal attitude to the border issue added insult to injury. The genesis of her relationship with immigrants was an incident that took place in a disused barn on the edge of the family's thirty-four acre farm, when Jen was eleven years old. She and her best friend, Mario, used it as a bolt-hole where they would sniff glue, play checkers, read pornographic magazines, and generally hang out.

One September afternoon they had been practicing wheelies on their bicycles and were lying on their backs, dreamily looking at the sky through the gaps in the broken roof slats. As she squinted upwards the small segments of puffy clouds appeared to Jen as floating sheep that had gone to heaven and were sublimely happy as they lounged around on their gravity-free blanket in the sky.

They suddenly heard a rustling noise and what sounded like a person coughing at the back of the cavernous, oval-shaped barn. All that separated them from potential danger were some very old, burnished, bundles of hay, the blackened edges of which looked like burnt pasta. Both of them were fairly freaked out and ready to get the hell out of there. But they recovered their composure. Each of them picked up a stick and crept towards the potential danger zone. What they found was a small, disheveled Hispanic man, who had blood seeping out of a bandana which was wrapped around a leg wound. The man's lips were as cracked as a shattered windscreen, and his hands and face were covered in mud. He was barefooted and had on a pair of khaki shorts and a yellow T-shirt on the front of which appeared the image of a tractor and the words: "Massey Ferguson." He was moaning softly and asking for "*agua.*"

Jen knew immediately that the man was "an illegal" because the existence of such people had been drummed into her for as long as she could remember. If she ever came across any, her parents told her, run away as fast as possible and inform them or any other family member she could find. They would likely be armed, dangerous, and Mexican. They were here for a free lunch and needed to be punished first and then sent back across the border. So why did she not immediately adhere to these instructions when just such a situation occurred? Probably partly because Mario had been with her and partly because she understood right away that the man posed no threat to her. Indeed, not only was he not a threat, but the children realized straight away that the man needed help, and quickly. They brought him water and cleaned him up. He would not or could not speak, but he looked at the kids with a mixture of gratitude and bemusement.

Maybe, Jen thought later, he understood that he owed them both his life and his destiny. For three days the child Samaritans nursed the man back to health, bringing him food parcels that they'd smuggled out of their homes and a bottle of whisky and some cloths for treating the wound. Jen had watched many Westerns in which alcohol was dabbed on open wounds. On the fourth night, wearing pants, shirt, and shoes that Jen had procured from the local dollar store and equipped with eight dollars in quarters and dimes that Mario had taken out of his piggy bank and a ham, cucumber, and mustard sandwich—Jen's father's favorite—the man left the ranch. He appeared sprightly and seemed to have some idea as to where he was going, because he'd pointed several times towards a power plant that lay ten miles to the west of the ranch, whose cream-colored chimney stacks on the horizon resembled silhouetted desert lighthouses.

Two years after the barn incident, a rancher called George Hanigan and his two sons abducted and tortured three Mexicans close to the town of Douglas, soon after they had crossed the border. Legal proceedings ensued and the episode became infamous, as well as sharply polarizing opinion. Jen's entire family sided with the Hanigans. The idea that they would be prosecuted for taking action against people who had no right to be in the country enraged them. Furthermore, because the government did next to nothing, vigilantism was entirely justified. Jen found herself taking the opposing position. What the Hanigans did was nothing more than racially motivated torture. It was barbaric and they should be sent to prison.

One evening, the family was discussing the case over dinner, and Jen's Uncle Mitchell, a Vietnam veteran who had the stars and stripes tattooed onto his neck, was letting rip. "Fuck those wetbacks, they had it coming, I tell you. Wish I'd been there. What the Hanigans did ain't nothing compared to what I would have done."

"Well said, Mitch." Jen's father and brother were all smiles, and they clinked their bottles of Budweiser together.

"You can't go around torturing people, Uncle Mitchell," said Jen. "After all, those Mexicans didn't threaten anyone, and they were only here for a better life." There was a stunned silence in the Williamson's living room. It was as though they'd all seen a ghost. Jen watched the collective hanging open of jaws. Not even a communist infiltrator could have incurred more wrath than Jen faced at that moment. And then all hell let loose.

"Why, you dirty traitorous rat. To think that a daughter of mine could spew such liberal claptrap." Her father smashed his clenched fist on the table. He also turned purple.

"She's been got at, damn it. I knew that Indian friend of hers was trouble," was her brother, Donald's reaction. "Good God, girl. You are seriously deviant if you believe that. I fought for this country to keep it safe from vermin like those spics. Commies are not welcome here, why should those parasites be?"

Uncle Mitch shook his head in disbelief for a good five minutes.

Mario and Jen were childhood friends, and if they'd been brother and sister they couldn't have been any closer. Indeed, Jen was a whole lot closer to him than she was to her only sibling, Donald, who was nine years older than she and worked with their father as a rancher. In the same class throughout their school years, Jen and Mario had the kind of shared history and instinctive understanding that proved that there were exceptions to the "blood is thicker than water" truism. In fact, they even decided when they were twelve that whoever died first would leave everything he or she owned to the other.

Mario was part Mexican, part Spanish, part Colombian, and part Pascua Yaqui. The Yaqui were Mexican Indians who'd lived for some fifteen hundred years alongside the Rio Yaqui, in Mexico's northernmost state of Sonora. They'd fought with the Spanish colonialists and, subsequently, on and off, for four hundred years, the Mexican government. At the onset of the twentieth century, they were ethnically cleansed by the Mexican dictator, Porfirio Diaz, and many fled north to Arizona. Their unpredictability led to them being viewed as either valiant renegades or cunning opportunists. They sided with the Americans against the Mexican general Santa Anna at the famous battle of the Alamo in 1836 and then, in 1911, they formed multiple allegiances during the Mexican War of Independence.

Mario was proud of his tribal roots, and he, Jen, and a small number of their closest friends would have annual gatherings where they took peyote and loosely acted out Pascua (the name of the land they settled in Arizona) Yaqui rituals. Mario always played the role of the Pascola dancer, the exuberant master of ceremonies, and he would wear a goat mask, containing the Yaqui symbols for the sun, and a sleigh bell belt which represented both the seven stars of the Big Dipper constellation and the original seven Yaqui villages by the Rio Yaqui.

Mario came into his own when he delivered the address at their unorthodox celebrations: "*Achai Taa*, Our Father, let me enter the sun with dignity and let me become a star and consult with the ancestors. Let me become wise like them and let me spread that wisdom among my kin. Let us gather the flowers that grew from Christ's blood, and let us scatter them so that they become more plentiful. We Yaqui-folks gave our own blood in the long fight against our oppressors, and now we offer up to the heavens the flames of the burning traitor, Judas. It is an aroma of praise to our Lord."

For her part, Jen assumed the role of the Deer Dancer, a great honor in Yaqui culture. The deer is a sacred animal for the Yaquis because at one time it was a crucial source of food for the tribe and its skin was greatly valued. She'd wear a red bandana, have deer antlers attached to either side of her head, and cocoon rattles tied to her ankles. She'd glide around in a ballet-like impersonation of the supple, Sonoran deer, after which she would call for an extended period of silence before delivering her speech. "We must administer a thorough beating to those long nosed *Chapayekas* and their cohorts, the Pharisees, who facilitated the crucifixion of the Son of God. Let them be killed by their own bloody swords, or, better still, let them be drowned in a sea of red flowers. Let us honor our beloved Virgin Mary. We would be satisfied if she bestows on us even a quarter of her divine purity. And let us pay tribute to the venerable Congressman Morris K. Udall to whom we owe our land and our sovereignty here in Arizona. Sir, we salute you and trust that you continue to roam free in the heavenly realm."

Their friends would holler, giggle, and whirl around like dervishes.

Mario's parents told him that the indentation that he and all of his twelve siblings had on the back of their skulls was a genetic trait due to their Basque ancestry. The propensity to suffer from insomnia which ran in the family was because of their Colombian blood, as was the flair for gambling. Their Mexican heritage had instilled in them the indispensable qualities of resilience and ambition in addition to a rather peculiar proclivity to want to breed pigeons. A well-honed survival instinct coupled with a warrior mentality was put down to Yaqui ancestry.

In Mario's family, there was an explanation for almost everything, although Mario couldn't help noticing that no one had ever sought to explain to him why it was that he was the only one in the family who was so partial to mind-altering drugs. He had often attempted to raise the issue but was never taken seriously. "Don't be silly, Mario," they would say. "We know that a boy as sensible as you would never throw away your life on such frivolous pursuits. Besides, how could your fragile body tolerate such abuse?"– this was a reference to his irritable bowel condition—"Anyhow, look at you, you're eating so well these days you'll soon be as fat as Popeye"—the family's prize rooster—"Hard drugs, no, not our Mario. Not *el uno especial*...." He'd earned this sobriquet after having been born two months premature and then surviving, apparently something of a rarity among the Mexican working class in the early sixties.

Mario was born in Nogales, Mexico and moved across the line to Nogales, Arizona when he was four. Then, at seven, he moved to Benson, before finally settling in Tucson when he was eighteen. His father was renowned as one of the best brickies in the region, and, by the time he was a young buck, Mario knew as much about bricklaying as Jen knew about ranching. Like Jen with ranching, Mario was not switched on by his father's trade, but he did find that he had a penchant for making things. When he was nine, he made a stainless steel fountain using the metal from old saucepans. True to his essence as a mestizo, Mario's skills and tastes were as eclectic as the colors in a bag of Skittles. He trained as a chef in Mexico City and as a tool and die machinist in Tucson. For many years, he'd provided catering services at Tucson's internationally renowned Gem and Mineral Show and supplied his own unique brand of brass smoking pipes and stash containers to 4th Avenue smoke shops.

Mild-mannered and a long-time pacifist, he was probably the last person on earth who anyone expected to own sixty-one guns. Indeed, his collection was, alongside his collection of twenty-four keyboard synthesizers, his pride and joy. It was apparently worth thirty-five grand. He said that he only carried a gun when he was on his bicycle "cos there's people out there who have mean dogs who go after cyclists." His favorite gun was a Chinese made Norinco MAK 90 which he'd paid around five hundred bucks for and was apparently now worth three thousand. What was special about it was its milled receiver which was made out of solid steel.

As for Jen, she was, in adulthood, decidedly chameleon-like. One day she'd appear as a raffish tomboy with short, peroxide hair, opaque, gothic-style makeup, army-surplus get-up, one cigarette dangling from her lips and another wedged behind her left ear. On another, she'd be sporting a suntan, a slinky, off the neck satin dress, six-inch heals, blue and gold speckled tights, and a chunky Bulgari watch.

She had a decidedly checkered history on the man front: four failed marriages and countless relationships ranging from twenty-four hours to eight years. She loved to joke about her disastrous love life. "There was a time when I'd married every guy I'd ever fucked. For some reason, I seem to get involved with members of the Lucky Sperm Club. The advantage is that they like their wives and children to drive Cadillacs, but the downside is that they're all as crooked as a barrel of snakes."

Alongside the odd stint on the ranch when her father was short-staffed, Jen had worked as a commercial realtor in Nogales, a bookkeeper in Douglas, a manager of a pawn shop in Benson, and a telephone salesperson in the advertising department of a newspaper in Tucson.

By the close of the twentieth century, Jen and Mario, the all-purpose pals, were both approaching their fourth decade and both itching for a new challenge. Right on cue, one came along. Mario's grandfather had owned a plot of land in the west of Tucson, adjacent to the now largely arid Santa Cruz River, in what was now called "Barrio Hollywood." He'd originally built a house on it, and, in the early fifties, the Koreans whom he sold the land to converted the ground floor into a liquor store. Since then, it had remained a liquor store but had been run by Iraqis twice, Palestinians and Mexicans, three times. The most recent owner, Salvador, was moving to Phoenix to open a restaurant and was looking for a quick sale. Twelve thousand for the goodwill and the stock seemed like a reasonable price. In the end, Jen and Mario paid ten grand in cash, and Mario threw in his Armalite AR-10, 308 caliber semi-automatic rifle. "What goes around comes around," said Mario, who never allowed himself to get too excited about anything. "It just feels right that it's back in the family again."

"Yee-ha," said Jill. "Let's kick ass." And she made her intentions abundantly clear by sprucing up the shop with plenty of flashing neon and changing its name from "Cut Price Liquor" to "Sip'n Slurp Booze."

"Sip'n Slurp Booze" soon became a hub in the Barrio Hollywood community. Folks would refer to it simply as "The Store," and it was the starting point for many hundreds of outings. Picnics were prepared, plans hatched, secrets divulged, rumors begun, and loves revealed. The fact that at least five marriage proposals, two births, one death, one stabbing, and a handful of arrests had happened on site during the eleven years of its existence only added to its legendary status. There were many Mexican customers, and they all knew that if they had a serious problem the partners would go the extra mile to try and solve it. Mostly they needed help when a member of their family had been seized and detained in an unknown location by *La Migra*—the stock Hispanic term that was used for immigration officers or if they themselves were feeling particularly insecure and wanted to go to ground for a while.

It could take a while, but Jen and Mario were usually able to find out where the individual was being held and then enlist the help of a refugee advocacy group, or, if they were very lucky, an immigration lawyer. About half the time the outcomes were positive—misunderstandings were cleared up, the relevant applications were submitted, expired papers were renewed—but there were often deportations and extended out-of-state detentions that they were powerless to prevent. Issues around The Border Crossing Card were particularly troublesome. Few holders of the card ever adhered to its conditions—to remain in the U.S. for no longer than thirty days and to remain within twenty-five miles of the border—and so many of them were stolen and forged that it was often impossible to determine who'd actually used one to cross. Jen and Mario knew three families who'd been separated due to Border Crossing Card violations, the deported parent being forced to leave his or her children behind.

Year after year Jen and Mario would hear horror stories about immigrants getting into trouble in and around the border at Nogales or Naco or Agua Prieta at the hands of *coyotes* and anti-immigrant vigilantes. After opening the store, they decided to try and do something about it. Jen, Mario, and five others formed a close-knit group of immigrant sympathizers. Every month, they would all put money into a kitty. The idea was that they would be ready to step in at the drop of a hat and rescue immigrants who needed help. It usually came down to money. If they paid the amount demanded by the other side they could take possession of the "goods."

Everything changed in April 2010 with the introduction of a draconian immigration law in Arizona, the infamous SB1070. A whole range of stakeholders were snared by its tentacles. It became a misdemeanor crime for a foreigner to not carry the required immigration documents on his or her person and for a person to hire, shelter, or transport illegals. And here was the really toxic bit: all law enforcement officers, in the course of a routine interaction with members of the public, were mandated to determine the immigration status of an individual should there be a reasonable suspicion that he or she is an illegal alien.

"This shit is serious, Mar," said Jen. "You do realize that if they catch us harboring or transporting we're well and truly fucked."

Mario, as ever, remained unfazed. "Stay cool, Jen Jen. We're sharper than they are. We're a well-oiled machine—they can't touch us. Here, have a go on this little spliff."

Jen cackled like a mother hen. "God, you're funny. You really do believe that you've got some divine ability to cruise under the radar forever and a day." The joint dangled from her mouth and she coughed hard before staggering to her feet, passing it back to Mario, opening the porch door, and spitting with great velocity on the ground.

"Oh that's charming. Thanks, Jen, just as I'm about to eat my fish taco. But you are a hard-as-nails tomboy so I guess you got a reputation to keep up," said William, their childhood friend.

"Jen Jen, you're forgetting something. The cops are fucking pissed about this new law. They all say the same thing: first of all, it's not our goddam job, and second, our relations with the community are gonna be screwed," said Mario.

"I hear you, Mar, but don't ever get too complacent about law enforcement. I mean, once they get the bit between their teeth all hell's gonna break loose."

"Hey guys, lighten up. It may just turn out to be a whole lotta hot air. By the way, do you remember the time outside that nightclub in Nogales when Jen turned around and smacked that fat guy in the jaw and he went down nice'n easy? You know, the cocky guy with the ponytail, who tapped her on the ass a couple times?" William had a memory like a steel trap and was always good value.

SB1070 shook the Latino community to its core. The fear was palpable. Many parents pulled their kids out of school, abandoned their homes, and went into hiding, in safe houses, in churches, in disused buses. There was a flood of Mexicans who made their way solemnly back across the border to Nogales, to Hermosillo, to Guaymas. It was a classic case of "from the frying pan into the fire" given the dreadful circumstances in their native country, a drug-war afflicted place where piles of bodies or heads or headless bodies were turning up with increasingly horrifying regularity. Jen and Mario were ready and swung into action. Food parcels, medical supplies, and, in the most pressing of circumstances, shelter, more often than not in a safe house in Oregon, were provided. Two families even begged them to sign power of attorney agreements to the effect that they would be the legal guardians of their U.S.-born children in the event that the parents were locked up or deported. It was a big commitment, even for them, but they did it.

Jen was right. Once the police were emboldened there was no stopping them. They certainly didn't back off when SB1070 was being challenged in the courts and was not technically enforceable. Nor did they when a federal court injunction stopped five of its main provisions.

Jen knew that as far as immigration was concerned things always ebbed and flowed. Sooner or later, a challenging situation always cropped up. And sure enough, no sooner had she placed her Sunday morning scrambled eggs on the kitchen table than Jen received a call from Lethargic Louis, an old acquaintance from Nogales, who was part of the group. "Jen, we got a situation and we need you and super Mario down here a-sap. Vince got a call. There's a coyote in one of the Grand Avenue drainage tunnels, and he's holding a Mexican guy and his son at gunpoint. Says the guy owes him seven hundred bucks and won't let them go until he gets it. Plus, the coyote's got an arm wound and needs some medication. I checked it out. The guy's super agitated. Jen. Can you be here this afternoon with the loot? I'll take you to the tunnel."

"Fuck me, Louis. There's five of you down there. You gotta be able to handle it between you. Where the hell's Vince?"

"He had to get his ass over to San Diego. His mom just had a stroke. They say it's bad. Charlie and Juan are still laying low in Hermosillo—you remember that problem we had with the crooked guy from ICE. Me and Sol are here but we only got three hundred and twenty in the pot. That pregnant woman in Agua Prieta who needed a C-section cost us an arm and a leg. Sorry, Jen, I know it's all messed up. We'll get the dough back, though."

"Jesus Christ, Louis, I'll be six feet under before your lot get your shit together." She sighed heavily. "Okay, we're on our way. But let it be known that Jen is not a happy camper."

Jen drove a BMW 525 and it always had a stars and stripes flag attached to the trunk and a "support our troops" sticker on the rear fender. And she always made sure she was listening to a shock-jock on the radio when she passed through a border checkpoint. She'd hollowed out space for two smallish adults or an adult and a child under the rear seats, and she always made sure to dump a whole lot of stuff in the back of the car and in the trunk. In the basement of the store, which was ideal because it was full of nooks and crannies, they had fitted out a room where folks could hide. The entrance was by way of a small hatch which was hidden behind a large chest. They only used it once or twice a year for very short periods.

Pepe, a building contractor from Ciudad Juarez, had built up his business over a five year period, and life for himself, his wife, and their two kids was half decent. And then he'd been offered "protection" by the local mafia who wanted fifty percent of the profits. He'd somehow held them at bay for six months. But they'd ratcheted up the pressure by trashing his office and making death threats. When they fired shots at his house, he understood he had to get the hell out. It was decided that he and his son would make their way to San Diego and his wife and daughter would go to Hermosillo. He'd bring them over later, when he'd set himself up in the States.

He was fully aware of the pitfalls of trying to relocate the whole family and start afresh in the United States. It was a high risk and could easily backfire, but he was so very down on his native country that he would've done almost anything to start afresh elsewhere. He'd seek advice in the Mexican community in San Diego. They would be bound to know a reliable lawyer. His wife begged him to join her in Hermosillo but he held firm. He didn't want to go there. Something bad would happen. You'd never be left in peace in Mexico. Besides, no one had any money there. He'd never be able to make ends meet.

Pepe agreed to pay the smuggler fifteen hundred dollars, half up front and half once they got to San Diego. Pepe gave the man seven-fifty, and his contact in San Diego would hand over the rest. He left his cash savings with his cousin, who advised him not to carry more than a few bucks with him. The smuggler reneged on the deal by dumping him in Nogales and insisting on being given the rest of the money. Pepe called his man in San Diego, who made a call to a guy in Lukeville, and the guy in Lukeville called Vince.

The tunnel was about three feet wide by no more than four feet high, and it was as close to hell as Jen and Mario had ever been. Airless, full of abandoned clothes, garbage, food, and feces, the smell was enough to make you puke. At the entrance they shone their torches and Mario pointed his gun. The coyote needed to know they were armed. He was lying on his side some twenty five feet away, waving a gun around and scowling. His hostages were sitting cross-legged against the wall. The boy looked no older than eight or nine. "*Calmate, hombre.* We got a gun, too. We'll give you five hundred bucks and some meds for your arm. Okay?" Mario shouted out.

There was no answer. The coyote was obviously thinking it over. After what seemed like ages, he replied, "Okay. But if you fuck around, we all die."

Mario reassured the man. "Nobody's gonna fuck around, man. There are better ways to die than in this stinking pit. Throw your gun towards us and we'll do the same. Then we'll come to you."

"How do I know I can trust you?" the coyote asked.

"Listen, dude, we're not dumb. Do you think we want every coyote in Mexico hunting us down?" said Mario.

Nothing happened for about ten minutes, but then the coyote slid his gun towards them. Mario did likewise. Crawling down the tunnel towards the coyote was definitely one of their most surreal experiences. As they drew close they saw a battered old man with a grey beard and a glass eye. There was blood oozing from an arm wound. He looked for all the world like a stand-in who really didn't want to be there. He may have seen better days, but he still had the steely look of a killer about him. He had droopy eyelids and a hawkish nose.

They were sizing each other up, and Mario was thinking that there was still the potential for things to go badly wrong when Jen let out an almighty shriek and began yelling out, "Fuck, I've been bitten. Son of a bitch. I think it was a rat."

The coyote made a move towards his gun, which lay on the ground about three feet away. Mario quickly reassured him. "*Hombre.* My friend got bitten by a rat. There's no problem." The guy made a face and muttered something under his breath but he relaxed. They gave him five hundred bucks and some bandages, Vicodin, and hydrogen peroxide. He looked Mario and Jen in the eye and they could feel the contempt. He then crawled back down to the Mexican end of the tunnel, grunting and wheezing as he did so. Surprisingly, he didn't ask for his gun back. Their charges watched the transaction intently, and, when the coyote had disappeared, hugged each other and broke down in tears. "He put the gun to my head, threatened to shoot me in front of my son," cried Pepe.

Jen and Mario understood that Pepe's situation was different from the other undocumented Hispanics they knew because shit had happened to him, and he had to get the hell out of Juarez. He may well be able to make an asylum application. They knew who to hook him up with, because that was their shtick really, networking, making good, reliable connections, knowing who to approach for whatever scenario presented itself.

"Hello, officer. How can I help you, sir?" Jen was all smiles and fluttered her eyebrows at the pudgy, avuncular officer, who already had it in his mind to return to the store as a customer when the SB1070 episode had blown over, which it inevitably would.

"Good morning. Are you Mrs. Williamson?"

"*Miss* Williamson if you don't mind."

"Oh, okay, sorry about that, *Miss* Williamson. I'm Officer Martinez. TPD. I'm sure you're busy so I'll get straight to the point. I know you're a person who's got her ear to the ground. Information, I mean good quality information, is always at a premium. And we're always interested in establishing friendly relations with the good folks in our community who are interested in making sure that, how shall I put it, things run as smoothly as possible."

Jen stopped smiling and fixed her gaze intently on the cop's jowly face. She would've loved to have laid into him but knew better than to antagonize law enforcement. "Well, officer, I very much believe in good community relations, as does my partner, Mr. Santa Anna, and we would always be happy to do our bit to promote harmony and understanding in our neighborhood. Of course, we have our regular customers who like to gossip. I usually know who's sleeping with who around here, but I guess that wouldn't particularly interest you." Jen laughed and Martinez joined her.

"You're funny, Miss Williamson. But I think you know what kind of information would interest us."

"Well, I assume you mean criminality, things like theft and assault and battery. I am right, officer?"

Martinez wasn't surprised. He'd been told Jen would be a tough nut to crack. But that was okay. He could wait. And he normally got what he wanted in the end. "Well, sure, all that good stuff is welcomed, but I was thinking more along the lines of border issues."

"Oh, I see. Gotcha. Well, okay, officer. It's not really something I know a whole lot about. I got plenty of Hispanic customers, but most of them have been here forever, and they spend so much time in church I doubt they got much time for wrongdoing. But sure, I hear a whisper and you'll be the first to know."

Martinez felt mildly irritated but left it at that. "Fine, Miss Williamson. Appreciate your time today. Be seeing you around."

Jen knew what Martinez's visit meant. If she played ball there would plenty of favors on offer. If she didn't, the gloves would come off. They were suspicious and would be watching her. They might even raid the store. But what was she going to do? Abandon everything she believed in for an easy life? No, no, and no again. Not the Tom Boy Border Rat, she thought. I've seen too many others sell out and then try and justify it to themselves or simply exist in a permanent state of self-denial. Whatever would be would be. But Jen Williamson would continue to live in the only way she knew how. Sometimes impulsive, even reckless, but always true. And always with a smile.

The Snake Charmer

Preening, prancing, pouting. Perfectly proportioned. Oozing panache. Here is a front man with a difference. The self-conscious swagger of a cocky John Travolta in Saturday Night Fever, the feline grace of Richard Gere in American Gigolo, and the infectious geniality of a slender young Sinatra in Guys and Dolls. On that basis, this young kid on the block could be forgiven for being as superficial as a politician's handshake and as hollow as his pledge. The Blue Heaven Nightclub in Tucson, a pristine venue in downtown Tucson, is where this slight, yet devilishly good-looking guy struts his stuff. He flits around, almost invisibly, and offers up the odd "Hello, how are you?" to new arrivals, delivered without intonation and not seeking a response. However, aside from aesthetic gratification, it is not exactly clear what his role is. Throughout the course of an evening his communication with the other staff is minimal.

While his interaction with the clientele is marginally greater, he affects aloofness as though it is a virtue to be flaunted. He's nowhere near big or menacing enough to be a bouncer—maybe he's a martial arts expert—nor is he magnetic enough to effectively seduce the club's savvy clientele. This man, I muse, inhabits an illusory twilight zone where what you see is most definitely not what you get. There's an imperceptible, edgy quality to him, unsettling yet indefinable.

I find myself inside a nightclub for the first time since my late twenties, at least ten years ago. I'm working on a scene in a novel I'm writing, in which a drug deal takes place. This place is very classily kitted out with blue and black tiger print carpets, beige 70s-style velour chairs and multi-colored halogen lighting. I'm alone, seated conspicuously in front of a huge 12' x 6' mirror. A halogen light burns directly into my shiny bald pate. I always try to sit near mirrors when I'm in bars and restaurants because they invariably enhance my voyeuristic experience. Unsurprisingly for a writer, I'm more than happy to sit and observe. It's my therapy. A cherubic, fresh-faced waitress, who has red dreadlocks and multiple nose and eyebrow studs, clears my table.

"Excuse me. I don't wish to be nosey, but that guy over there, by the entrance,

what's his job?"

"Oh, you mean Hassan. He's our doorman slash security guy. From Morocco. Not typical is he?"

"Not at all. I guess he's a martial arts expert or something. I mean, I'm guessing he doesn't go in for brute force."

"Actually, he's a pacifist and he's got special powers."

I'm unable to discern even the faintest hint of irony on the waitress's face.

"Oh, what sort of special powers?" I enquire eagerly.

"Basically, he can calm people down who are aggressive and about to become violent. He seems to be able to take the heat out of situations," she says.

"Really? How intriguing. Have you seen him do it?"

"Of course. We all have. Since he started working here we've had no trouble at all. Hassan's a Godsend. Truly, some kind of miracle." She seems genuinely in awe of the great man.

"So how does he actually do it?" I ask.

"Why don't you ask him yourself?"

"Well, are you sure he won't mind?"

"I'm sure you can sweet talk him into it." She smiles and touches my arm.

I look over at Hassan, who's sizing himself up in front of a small mirror on the wall adjacent to the front door. He's tall, I reckon close to 6 foot, has classically high cheekbones, and thick eyebrows that join up in the middle. Puckering his lips, he runs his hands through his silky black hair. I decide to go for it and approach this talismanic narcissist with a touch of trepidation.

"Excuse me, Hassan, sorry to bother you but your colleague over there said I should have a word with you." Hassan looks at me directly and then at my reflection in the mirror, but doesn't speak.

I continue even though the vibe is not good. "You see, I'm a freelance writer and would be interested in interviewing you to find out more about your special gift."

146

"My gift?" Hassan narrows his eyes.

"Yes, I understand you have the ability to calm people down, to defuse potentially explosive situations."

"Could be, but this is not good place for a chat. Come to Sahara Café on Prince Road. I am there every Wednesday night in October." And with that he swivels on his heels and walks away.

Three weeks later, I find myself sitting on a striking multi-patterned, red, white, black, and green colored sofa in the cozy hookah lounge at Safari Café, at Prince and Campbell. A wall-mounted flat screen TV shows Arabic pop music videos. The rhythms of East and West coalesce to good effect, and I soon find myself rocking back and forth. An eclectic bunch of fifteen or so customers are present. These include two Middle Eastern men smoking hookah pipes, a scholarly looking man in a crumpled white linen suit, and a group of giggly girls. A pony-tailed server wearing brown dungarees adds to the mix.

After an hour or so, we are all ushered outside to the courtyard. There's a stage area, the backdrop to which is a huge wall painting of the Sahara desert. Browns, blues, and reds are juxtaposed in bold brush strokes. A line of five miniature camels make their way along a sand dune. Another flat screen TV is mounted on the wall, and disco lights bounce across the concrete floor with all the levity of carefree hummingbirds. The music stops and the host, a middle-aged man with a toothy grin and prodigious sideburns, steps forward. He's wearing a fez and is elaborately attired in a white frilly shirt, black jacket adorned with gold braiding and tasseled epaulettes, black trousers, and leopard skin shoes.

"Gentlemen and ladies, we proudly welcome you to our Sahara heaven. Later on, our own music group, Khalil and the Casbah, but before, a special show. Here he is. Only he appears for you at Sahara in Tucson. Exclusive promotion for your delight. We have great pleasure to introduce the one and the only, Mr. Hassan and Rudolf, the rattlesnake."

The compere stands aside and begins to orchestrate a round of applause. Hassan comes out from the hookah lounge. He's transmogrified from slick, Moroccan dandy to pared down Eastern man. He's wearing a turban and loose fitting loincloth and is barefoot. He places the wicker basket he's carrying carefully on the stage, lifts the lid off, and sits down, cross-legged, facing it. The compere steps forward, swoops up the lid, and hands Hassan a wooden recorder. Hassan places it to his lips, and seconds later an elegiac, reedy sound floats across the room. The snake charmer is beginning to weave his magical spell. Right on cue the head of a snake appears above the parapet. Edging upwards by way of sinuous lateral movement, the glassy-eyed reptile is as graceful as a willow swaying in the wind. Once fully extended the snake holds its position momentarily. My eyes slide up and down its scabrous, banded, brown, and beige three-foot trunk. Hassan's eyes are shut, and he's as still as the snake. He begins to circumnavigate the basket ever so slowly, first clockwise and then counter-clockwise. Hassan and the snake gyrate their bodies in tandem. It's a perfect synergy. Now he subtly employs a marginally slower tempo, which appears to prompt the snake's descent. Having orchestrated it smoothly back into its basket, Hassan bows modestly and sits down again, adopting the same cross-legged posture. He sits, as still as a dinghy on the Dead Sea, eyes shut, for at least five minutes. As we wait, the sound system offers up some more haunting Eastern music. And then, Hassan repeats the process. Something seems different about the second part, but I can't put my finger on it. And then I realize it's not the same snake. This one's darker in color and is not banded. Jeez, the snakes are sharing the workload—that's even more impressive.

Hassan exits to enthusiastic applause. How cleverly he has reinvented his public persona in this altogether different milieu, I'm thinking. No longer the phlegmatic arrogance. Rather, a beguiling air of modesty and warmth. But the sense of mystery, of something not revealed, remains. A while later Hassan comes back out and is seated in front of the rock-filled fountain. The girls are making a fuss of him. One of them slips a piece of paper into his pocket. I wait for an opportune moment before initiating a dialogue.

"I'm Jason. We met at Blue Heaven a few weeks ago."

"Yes, I remember, you are journalist, right?" he asks.

"No, not a journalist, a freelance writer."

"Isn't it similar?" His eyes are an exquisite green and hazelnut color.

"Well, I write longer articles for magazines. I don't do stuff for newspapers."

"Oh, okay. I am a little suspicious of journalists. One time, one of them gave me small problem." Hassan briefly looks as though he's replaying past events in his mind.

"Anyway, really liked the act," I say. "Where did you pick up the art of snake charming?"

"My neighbor in Casablanca taught me. Mehdi. He was big character. He used to roll marbles along floor, and snakes went and collect them and bring back to him. One time I even saw snake which was wrapped around him suck his whole T-shirt over his head and into its body."

"But is there no risk at all? Aren't they venomous?"

Before he has a chance to answer we are joined by the host.

"Welcome, sir. What do you think of this main attraction?" The host eases himself down stiffly onto a bar stool. He grunts as he does so and is breathing heavily.

"Marvellous. I was absolutely spellbound," I say with unabashed gusto.

"Yes. He's a gold nugget. Actually, we try to organize a tour around the country for our star. You think Yankees will like him?"

"I can't think of any reason why not. It's not as though snake charming is a common sight in this country. I think he'll be a real novelty."

"Yes, that's right. We want to put him together with couple of other acts, maybe a juggler and Houdini man. But of course, Hassan is the main one."

"Very good. Put me down for the premiere, please."

"Excuse me. Selim. When you going to discuss with me about this tour? I do other jobs you know." Hassan winks at me as he feigns mock indignation. Nice to see him brighten up, I think.

"Young man. Nothing happens without you giving a green light. Let me reassure you, Mr. Hassan, your future as a super and extraordinary entertainer is safe with me. I am your path to gold and riches." Now it is Selim's turn to grin broadly at me as he seeks to appease his charge.

"I'm a freelance writer. Could I tag along for a week or so once you manage to get the tour up and running?"

"Why not, sir? As long as you don't sell us down the river. But you could not do that anyway, because people who sell down the river end up at the bottom of it, don't they, Hassan?" Selim roars with laughter at his own joke. The last time I'd heard a roar as deep and throaty as that was on safari in Tanzania's Serengeti plains, as I watched a male lion climax.

I'm lucky enough to have experienced Hassan the snake charmer in action but am obviously going to have to be patient in my quest to find out more about Hassan the mollifier. I am determined to witness him pacifying a potential violator of the peace, and, rather like a safari goer hoping for a sighting of the elusive cheetah, I pitch up at Blue Heaven on several occasions over the next month or so. I draw blanks but after four or five fruitless journeys I finally strike gold. As I arrive one Saturday night Hassan is being confronted by a belligerent man in a full-length black leather coat and pointy black boots, reinforced with steel toe and heel caps.

"Listen up, buster," he's saying. "I don't care what your stupid rules are. I'm meeting someone here and intend to go inside. So, are you going to move aside or would you like me to do it for you?"

Hassan looks the man straight in the eye but says nothing. He remains perfectly still.

"Well, what do you say? I don't have all day." The man appears slightly unsettled by Hassan's lack of response. Hassan leans forward and whispers something in his ear. As he does so he offers the man a glimpse of his inside jacket pocket.

The man looks pensive. Is it my imagination or does the color drain from his face?

"Tell you what, I'll check back a bit later." He turns on his metal clad heel and departs the scene. Hassan remains impassive but one or two of the bystanders are left open-mouthed. An hour or so later I manage to grab a moment with Hassan. "What did you say to him? I bet there's a snake in your jacket pocket, right?" He smiles broadly.

"Let's just say this. It's all to do with turning aggression into fear. They see inside themselves like never before and they are tamed." And that's all I get out of him.

A week or so later, on a Wednesday, I return to Blue Heaven. Selim is there but not Hassan. "Hassan not around, Selim?"

"No, Jason, he's not in circulation these days."

"You mean he's on a vacation?"

"I wish he was. No, he's in the jail somewhere in California."

"Holy cow. What the hell did he do?"

"Apparently he was involved in illegal trading of exotic animals. Something about snakes that went missing from the Royal Palace in Morocco and ended up in Sacramento."

"Shit, that sucks big-time," I say, in the absence of anything more profound to contribute.

Selim is genuinely upset. "It's very bad news for us. I worry for him in those places. He is too pretty. The tour will be delayed, but I wait for my brother. Nothing more to do." He shakes his head ruefully, and I notice that his eyes are moist.

Three months later and I'm sitting opposite Hassan in the visitors' area of California State Prison in Sacramento. He was sentenced to eighteen months for illegal importation of exotic pets. He's wearing blue dungarees and an orange high-visibility prison vest. His head is shaved and his cheeks are pretty hollowed out. He also has one hell of a shiner.

"So what happened? Did you do it?"

"I did do it and I deserve my punishment. I was big fool. I always thought of myself as streetwise guy, but I let this conman persuade me to go Morocco to get six snakes. He told me they had been bought by a US collector and that he had all the permissions from the Moroccan government. He said he needed someone who was snake expert to deliver them to new owner in Sacramento. He offered me five grand. Turns out the snakes were full of long pencil bags of cocaine. FBI discovered smuggling ring and were at the airport to meet me."

"So how come they didn't do you for drugs offences?"

"I was lucky. The jury accepted my story that I had no knowledge about drugs and had been used by the suppliers because I was snake expert. What an idiot I am."

"But how were you to know? Presumably the snakes were the genuine article."

"They were, except they were smelling very strange, like boiled vegetables, and I couldn't understand what it was."

"Selim mentioned the Royal Palace in Morocco."

"That's right. Apparently, snakes belonged to King's cousin and were stolen from the palace. This is big irony because of my background."

"Sounds intriguing, Hassan. Tell me."

"When I was baby my Dad was a valet at the palace. Something happened. I still don't know exactly what it was, but my Dad was accused of stealing some rare gemstones. At one moment it looked like he was going to be put on trial and could maybe face execution, but, luckily, we had wealthy relative who paid bribe and we were thrown out of country. Just left in desert on border with Algeria."

"Oh my God. What a nightmare."

"It really was. Anyway, for years we wandered around like nomads in border region but finally we found ourselves back inside Morocco. At the age of eleven I began working on a banana plantation."

Hassan goes quiet and scratches his head so hard that he creates red tracks that look like a kid's crayon scribbling. A minute or so later he emerges from his reverie. "In my life, the truth is always strange. You could not imagine stories like my own reality."

"It certainly makes my existence seem drab. But tell me about the banana plantation."

"Well, it's tough job. There is huge structure covering bananas made of rows and rows of metal poles covered by three layers of a thin material, like silk. There was a silk floor quite high up near roof. The hardest thing was learning to walk on this floor. You fall over for two or three days and then you learn to keep your balance. There is complicated process called the Banadero. It is funny. I often have nightmare dreams about being trapped inside one of those banana houses, surrounded by metal poles and layers and layers of silk. I am being chased by lion. It is terrible."

"Sounds very claustrophobic."

"Yeh, it was, but not as bad as being locked up in here."

"Sure, sure. So when did you come over here, Hassan?"

"Twelve years ago I met my ex-wife in Casablanca. She's from New York. We lived in Big Apple for eight years. Then we split and I came out here to link with Selim."

"What went wrong, Hassan?"

"Nothing too bad actually. Just we went separate paths. Time passed, we changed. That is all. We still speak. She is good lady, social worker. What about you, Jason? You married?"

"No. I managed four years but it ended badly. Mine stole twelve grand from me and ran off with my cousin."

"Shit. Really sucks, friend. But you are big man. I know you can conquer hurtfulness of love." Hassan pats me on the back.

"Thanks, Hassan, appreciate the kind words."

I visited with Hassan in the slammer twice more before his release. He was pretty good company for someone who was incarcerated. He'd certainly acquired that American "glass half-full" mindset. He appeared to resume life as a snake charmer and anger assuager without so much as a blip. Selim had enlisted some other acts, and they began to take the show on the road. As I got to know Hassan, he regaled me with ever more interesting stories of his early life. Apparently, in his teens he had stowed away on a cargo ship full of items as disparate as teddy bears and potpourri, light shades, and washing powder. The crew had discovered him sleeping in a basket of potpourri. He smelt like the inside of a beauty parlor for a month. As a child, he'd also travelled around Morocco as a shoeshine boy. On one occasion he'd gotten into an argument with an American diplomat in a pinstriped suit, who'd complained that Hassan had done a sub-standard job. Hassan ended up breaking his stool over the man's head. The diplomat complained, and Hassan spent a week in the police cells.

On an afternoon in early spring Hassan and I are strolling along the grassy expanse of The Mall on the 380 acre University of Arizona Campus. I'm an alumnus, and I want to show Hassan where I spent three of the happiest years of my life. We pass the elegant Herring Hall, HQ of the Campus Arboretum, boasting its beige, neo-classical portico, and the fabulous Stevie Eller Dance Theater, a glass building whose front façade is encased in a woven, wire mesh to create a crumpled, accordion effect.

I show him the Woman's Plaza, where I used to read Plato under the shadow of the sycamore trees. It has colored leaf tiles containing the names of honorees, integrated into the sidewalk, impressionistic Three Muses fountains, and seat-walls, along the center of which run tiled strips full of intricate, brightly colored art and pithy quotations. One by Mother Teresa reads: "We can do no great things, only small things with great love."

Hassan recounts, fairly lightheartedly, how, in his late teens, he dipped his toes into the world of petty crime: a bit of shoplifting here, some car theft there, all relatively benign. But then his mood abruptly changes. He seems distant and is looking down at his feet. He tells me something very shocking. I'm not even sure he means to tell me; it's almost as if the story is careering out of him involuntarily. Hassan had broken into the house of a very old, frail woman, who'd caught him red-handed. Whether gutsy or foolhardy, she'd come at him with her walking stick. He'd punched her in the stomach and watched in horror as she fell forward in slow-motion and cracked her skull open on the concrete floor. There was blood everywhere. He got out of there immediately. Ever since, he's been wracked with guilt and often wakes up gasping for air after dreaming that her blood is gushing over his head.

"Did you not think to call for an ambulance?" I ask him. "You could have remained anonymous."

"I know it. I know it. I was young. I couldn't think straight. I just ran and ran and then collapsed under a tree and slept. The next day, I took bus to Tangier. I stayed there more than one year before returning to Casablanca. I never heard anything about it on the news. But she did die. I am sure of it." We sit on a bench and Hassan, openly crying, continues his confession. "I could not keep it inside me any longer, Jason. You cannot imagine the hell of living with this event. I am killer. Every time I look at my face in mirror I see a killer. I put on act outside but it is just cover up. When you see me look at myself in nightclub it is like ... I don't know, like I pray that I can just one time see what everyone else sees. Believe me. Twice, I nearly put myself to death. Once I cut myself, and another time I took too many pills. Many times I thought to go back to Casablanca and confess. But I am coward. I cannot live in prison, better to die for me. God is punishing me even if humans have not done it. To have such a black conscience is the darkest thing in world. When I married and came to New York, I felt better, but still this devil thing was inside me. Many times I tried to tell Maria but I could not do it. How could I tell her who I really was? She would have been too devastated. But I felt, still I feel, like a fake man, my secret is eating my soul, day by day. Finally, I will just die. I am sure of it."

We sit in silence for quite a while, Hassan sobbing quietly. I'm shocked that he's revealed everything to me. After all, we haven't spent that much time together. My instinctive reaction is that I wish I didn't know anything about it. I'm struggling to know what to say to him. I offer a few words of consolation. Now that he's confided in me, confessed to another person, he will hopefully be on the path to peace of mind. The mental anguish will surely abate.

As the weeks go by, I just can't get the Hassan thing out of my head. He's a murderer, it seems, and that fact alone is unsettling. Knowing one murderer makes you analyze everyone you meet in terms of whether they may have killed. I'm developing some unhealthy suspicions about a neighbor of mine but that's another story. I keep picturing Hassan punching that old woman and her skull cracking apart on a cold concrete floor. I would certainly not like to have lived my life burdened by that degree of guilt. I try hard to empathize with him but find it hard. Yes, he was young and did something terrible that he's regretted every minute of his life. But the bottom line is that he took a life and there's nothing worse, nothing. On the two occasions I've seen Hassan I've found it difficult to be in his company. I think I've managed to disguise my feelings, but he's not the same Hassan, he never will be. He hasn't mentioned the subject again and has shown no outward sign of being troubled.

I have no way of knowing whether he regrets spilling the beans to me. But what to do or not do? Should I just let it go? After all, it has nothing whatsoever to do with me. It's information which was given to me in confidence, by a friend, about an event that happened many years ago, half way across the world. Surely I should just consign it to a storage unit within the deepest recesses of my brain. But maybe not. If I don't act, do I not become complicit myself? Aren't I morally bound to pass on such information to law enforcement? That old woman must have had a family who were, or are still, seeking justice. I put what I described as a hypothetical scenario to three acquaintances. Predictably, one said act, one said do nothing, and the third was as uncertain as I was.

There were two deciding factors. One was that I'd long been seduced from afar by Morocco's charms, not least its medieval kasbahs and spice-laden souks. And the other was that I'd started dabbling in travel-writing, having visited Croatia and Latvia and written pieces on them. So a dual-purpose trip to Morocco became a firm plan. While traversing the country as a tourist and travel writer, intent upon attuning my senses to its multifarious essences, I also resolved to make discreet enquiries about the killing of an old woman in Casablanca many years earlier. As I slumber on the first leg of my three-flight journey from an Old Pueblo in North America to an equally old kingdom in North Africa, I wonder whether my pursuit is not simply the self–indulgent pursuit of a footloose and fancy free writer or whether it might actually turn out to be something whose ramifications are of a permanent and deadly serious nature.

I am immediately smitten by Casablanca, a perfect mélange of the modern and the mystical, the Medina and the Mosque, the souk and the sea. A panoply of huge, sumptuous, white, Arabo-Andalucian colonial buildings, some crumbling in a distinctly Havanaesque way, dominate the urban landscape. There are also a good few art deco structures --not least an art deco cinema/theater building called The Rialto. Right away I envisage a Tucson Rialto—Casablanca Rialto cultural exchange. Named eponymously after the country's penultimate King, is the gargantuan Hassan 11 Mosque, with its two hundred foot high minaret, which apparently took thirty-five thousand workers and seven years to build. Having been constructed on a promontory which juts out spectacularly into the Atlantic, its size and opulence place it firmly within the pantheon of indulgencies which have borne the hallmark of monarchs and absolute rulers throughout history.

I experience the teaming old Medina, with its mountains of Technicolor spices and carpets and rugs draped over every available edifice, a huge collage stretching up into the clear blue sky. A far cry from my corn-fed, shopping-malled country, I'm thinking. The couscous and lamb kebabs are heavenly, but I give the goats' brains a wide berth. And then I come upon a gaggle of snake charmers. Maybe this was where Hassan learned his trade. Most of them looked young, but there was one older guy. Should I ask him if he knew Hassan? Nothing to lose so I approach and show him a photo of Hassan. He takes a look but shakes his head blankly. My main plan is to approach the local newspapers. There may be something in their archives. I've got precious little information, and I know it's a longshot but you never know.

The first three papers, two in Arabic and one in French, yield absolutely nada. I try another local French paper called Aujourd'hui Le Maroc. I walk up five flights of narrow, winding stairs and find myself in a smoke-filled room which is lined from wall to ceiling with newspapers. A smartly dressed middle-aged man with curly grey hair, reading glasses propped on the end of his nose and a cigarette dangling from his lips, is bashing away on an old typewriter. I stand watching him for some thirty seconds. Without stopping or looking up, he says, in English, "Can I elp you?" I enquire whether he has any recollection of an attack on an old woman which happened about seventeen or eighteen years ago. A man broke into her house and punched her. She fell on a concrete floor and may have been killed. He stops typing, takes his cigarette out of his mouth, and looks up at me. "Well, don't you ave even a name of zee victim, sir, or any detail about zee location?" I shake my head. "I sink zees is imposseeble wiv zee lack of information, but I ave one sing I need to check. Come back tomorrow."

Twenty-four hours later I'm sitting opposite the man. My eyes are stinging. The scene is identical, reading glasses still propped, cigarette still dangling. Without speaking, he hands me a crinkly old newspaper, opened at page fourteen and with three short paragraphs ringed. I read it and, pleased that my schoolboy French seems to still be intact, think the first sentence says that a sixty-six year old woman, Madam Le Farvre, was assaulted by a thief in her home and is in a serious condition in hospital. The paper is dated March 10, 1994.

The man, who introduces himself belatedly as Mr. Djellaba, explains that this was one of a spate of robberies around Casablanca of houses owned by elderly people. This particular woman is said to have sustained multiple wounds and to have been in a serious but stable condition. He distinctly remembers the robberies being reported. If he is not mistaken there was an oddity in that the perpetrator or perpetrators would always take exactly half of whatever cash they found. Mr. Djellaba is pretty sure that no fatalities ever resulted. And he doesn't think that anyone was ever caught. "Thank you, Mr. Djellaba, that's very useful. I am grateful." I feel immediate relief to find out that, in all probability, Hassan is not a killer. How and why he was so convinced that he had done for the old lady is an interesting question. Mr. Djellaba lights a fresh cigarette with the butt of the one he's just smoked. "So, Mr. Jason, what is your eenterest in zis matter?"

"Forgive me, Mr. Djellaba, if I don't go into the details. It's a little bit delicate."

"Ah, yes, yes, I quite understand. Gozeep can be dangerous, no? We ave a saying in Le Moroc. One man's gozeep is another man's last breathe." He chuckles in a suitably sinister fashion, exposing his black teeth in the process.

On the flight home, I sip my scotch on the rocks and reflect happily on a mission more or less accomplished. If not a definitive result, I feel I have enough information to at least try and provide some comfort to Hassan. Worst case scenario, there's no quelling his deeply rooted angst, and he may react badly to my meddling in his affairs. But that's a risk I'm prepared to take. My motives are honorable and that's all that's important. I shut my eyes and feel the North African sun on my back as I stroll along La Corniche, Casablanca's waterfront promenade. I drift off and images of blood gushing and snakes and old women, all shrouded in cigarette smoke, enter my head.

Debt Conversion

The shrill sound of the telephone interrupted Adam's fitful sleep. He instinctively reached out for the phone without opening his eyes but found himself clutching at thin air. He levered his unwilling body up and to the left. His throat was parched and he was already irritable. "Who the fuck could this be?" he said out loud as he looked at the clock. "It's 8 o'clock on a Saturday morning."

Adam grabbed the phone. "Hello." His tone was gruff and uncompromising.

"Is that Adam Pritchard?" said a man's voice.

Adam knew at once that it was one of his creditors. He thought of pretending to be someone else but what was the point? These people were persistent, and they would just call again and again until they got hold of you.

"Yes."

'Good morning, Mr Pritchard, I am calling from Capital One Bank. For security reasons can I have the last four of your social?"

"3876. Look, is this really necessary? I spoke to one of your colleagues three days ago."

"Sorry, sir. There is nothing showing on my computer about a recent conversation, and we haven't received any payments from you for over six...."

"Buddy, as I told your colleague, I'm not in a position to make any payments until the end of the month. I propose to send you a check for 50 bucks on the 30th, okay?"

"Well, your account is delinquent in the amount of $475, and you would need to make a minimum payment of $100 today and further agree to make monthly payments to avoid legal proceedings."

"That's impossible. I can't afford that much."

"What can you afford, sir?"

"I already told you. Nothing until the 30th, but I could maybe stretch to $75 and then $75 a month from then on."

"The $75 monthly may work, sir, but we must insist on a payment today. I could spea...."

"Look, how many times do I have to tell you people?" Adam's decibel level began to rise. "I'm flat-assed broke and a payment today is impossible."

"There's no need to shout at me, sir."

"I'm not shouting," said Adam, shouting.

"Sir, you will need to calm yourself down. Otherwise we will not be able to continue this discussion."

"You know what, that's the best idea you've had today. Let's terminate this conversation as it's starting to really piss me off."

"Very well, sir, I'll have to place the matter in the hands of our legal department."

"Fine, whatever." Adam slammed the phone down. His heart was beating heavily, and his stomach had tightened up. He flopped back into bed, thoroughly drained and full of angst. He lay prostrate and stared up at the blank ceiling. He felt utterly numb. I might as well have cancer, he thought, because that's exactly what debt is, a cancer. It creeps up on you without warning, destabilises, overwhelms and, finally, paralyses you. Once it has taken possession of you it ruthlessly batters you into submission. It knows no mercy nor does it tolerate any weakness. It swamps you with self-pity and whips away your dignity. Like cancer, it can lay dormant within you, a latent menace, while the seeds of doom are planted. It may even suggest itself to you but always subliminally, at one remove. When you think you have it beaten it creeps back surreptitiously and corners you again, often fatally. It is corrosive, a plague on the heart. You can no longer love, and you withdraw inside yourself in an orgy of despair, hiding from those who would give you succour.

Adam had given up his telesales job at Geico to set up a wholesale clothing company, but the timing had been awry and he went belly up, along with an untold number of other small businesses which were caught up in the 21st century's first great depression. Adam was no expert on economics, but the fallout from the banking crisis, the evidence of which he saw all around him, sure felt a lot worse than a standard boom and bust recession. He'd never seen so many middle class folks lose their homes, quite a few of whom actually become reliant on food stamps.

The experience had put a huge dent in his carapace of self-confidence. For months Adam preoccupied himself with debt reconstruction and consolidation packages. He didn't care how many people advised him to cut his losses and go bankrupt, Adam Pritchard was determined not to allow society to stigmatize him. As he sank further and further into the quicksand, he began to face up to the fact that his juggling act could no longer be sustained. The truth was painful, and all Adam's trusty resolve began to ebb away. Determination turned into despair and vigour into lethargy.

Saturday afternoon Adam drifted aimlessly amidst the throngs of people at Park Place Mall, immersed in a multitude of self-pitying thoughts. How could it all have gone so wrong? Had he made mistakes? Maybe he wasn't as good as he'd always thought he was. He pushed his way through a melee of high school students who were milling around expectantly as they waited for a chance to sit at the wheel of a gleaming new red Porsche which was being showcased. Adam slumped down onto an accommodating leather sofa and observed them laughing and joking. A chubby boy with curly blonde hair and red cheeks was chewing bubble gum. He would go up to other kids, blow bubbles close to their faces, and then back away quickly as they tried to burst the bubble. Such joie de vivre, such innocence. He genuinely hoped that twenty years down the road they wouldn't end up like him: morose and self-obsessed. Adam felt so very heavy; it was as though his own starter motor had short-circuited and drained all the dynamism out of his body. He had no idea how long he had been lounging there, deep in thought, when he heard a voice over a loudspeaker. He ventured outside to investigate.

"Come on, folks
Don't be a sinner.
Team up with Jesus
And be a winner.
Come with our merry little band,
we have been chosen,
to the Promised Land."

The man, who looked to be in his forties, was wafer thin and had tangled ginger hair. His face was deeply lined and covered in freckles. Most striking were his bright emerald green eyes. He wore a grey string undershirt, knee length shorts and sandals. In his right hand was a loudspeaker and in his left, a bible. A sprinkling of people listened to him, some with vacant bemusement, others displaying signs of enthusiasm. An elderly, slightly stooped man, in a brown pinstriped suit and matching brogues, whose collar was covered in specs of dandruff, nodded vigorously.

Adam wasn't sure if the man irritated or amused him. He hung around and, at an opportune moment, asked him, "Is it legal to use one of those?" Adam pointed to the loudspeaker.

"Of course it is, my friend. Is it legal to disobey the word of God? Did our Lord Jesus Christ die in vain? Will we not accept that we are sinners and take the path to eternal life?"

"How long have you been preaching?" asked Adam.

"Ever since I was saved, brother. Lazarus himself could not have ended up sprightlier than me. I was set free to sprinkle the Lord's magic potion all around. Catch me if you can—I'm the divine greyhound."

There was definitely an aura around this man, and Adam had to admit that he found his sales patter engaging. There was no messianic fervour, rather a mellifluous tone and a flow of well-chosen words which impacted with all the delicacy of snowflakes floating gently to ground.

"We're taking a trip soon. We are to be cleansed in Christendom's holiest waters. Come with us," ventured the preacher.

"Thanks for the offer, but I don't think it's my scene. In any case, I'm the world's worst traveller. You know, fussy eater, hygiene freak."

"Friend, let me take you by the hand,
And lead you to the Promised Land,
Cast aside the lethargy of doubt
Come and seek sanctuary in the world without."

"Why are you even asking me to come with you? I only met you five minutes ago, and you know absolutely nothing about me?" Adam responded indignantly.

"Oh, but I do know about you. You were coiled like a serpent over there.

Alone in the desert, the sun beating down on your back. Exposed and vulnerable, you were rooted to that spot, the force of gravity upon you."

"Excuse me! You've got a lot of nerve, buddy. Psycho-analyze me, why don't you?"

The preacher remained silent but looked at Adam knowingly.

"Anyway, it's been good meeting you but I've got to go."

The preacher called out as Adam beat a hasty retreat.

"If you change your mind I'll be here at the same time next week. The name's Westerby by the way. Just call me Arnie."

All the way home, Adam could not get the divine greyhound out of his mind. Why should a chance meeting with an eccentric evangelical Christian strike such a resonant chord? Like pretty much everyone else in his secular family, Adam had no faith. He had always considered himself an earthy type, practical and straight talking. He knew that millions of his fellow citizens were, to a greater or lesser extent, believers. And that was fine, provided they didn't bother him. As it was, you could barely go through a day in Tucson without seeing an advertisement for God or his son, either on a wall or the back of someone's car. He'd had one or two brief conversations on his doorstep with Jehovah's Witnesses who'd tried to convert him. He seemed to recall that they'd talked about some kind of paradise on earth, where the sun always shined and sheep and cows grazed in your back yard. He remembered saying sarcastically that that sounded deathly boring to him. He'd rather stick with this world, in which the unexpected might and usually did happen.

Why he should suddenly be drawn towards a bible thumper now was a mystery to him. True, he was in a rut. He lacked direction and was too stubborn to seek out a friendly shoulder to cry on. He'd been down on his luck before but always managed to summon from within the necessary resolve to get back on track. For the first time in his life Adam found himself reaching out for external assistance. He began to question whether or not there really might be a God or a life after death.

Adam returned to Park Place Mall the following Saturday. He wanted to see if the preacher man was there and whether he would still have the same effect on him. Perhaps the heat of the sun and the strange feeling of disorientation that had afflicted him that day had had something to do with it. Adam had no difficulty whatsoever locating him in exactly the same place as the last time, next to the coin filled fountain outside the main entrance. As he approached, God's messenger was quick to spot him and, breaking away from a gaggle of prospective neophytes, was quickly into his stride. "Ah, hello again. Have you returned to follow the instructions of Jesus? Stand and testify, friend. Do not hide any longer. Come forth and allow your heart to mend. Let yourself be immersed in the holy water. Rise again, good man, as did our Messiah, up you will go, higher and higher."

"Look, fella, I can't deny I like the sound of what you say, but it's like trying to decipher a riddle. Can't you just spell it out for me in layman's terms?"

"It's all in the book, mister. Man cannot stand alone, however good he is. No, sir, only complete faith in the Son of Man can save his soul. It is written: 'A man is not justified by the works of the law, but by the faith of Jesus Christ.' Examine yourself, establish your own righteousness, and you too will be rewarded with eternal life."

Adam was beginning to get a feel for what this eccentric apostle was saying. "So, erm, do you mean that what I do will not make any difference to my destiny?"

"That's it friend. Be humble. Expect no divine reward for your actions. Completely trust Jesus and from that moment you are saved...forever."

"I see," said Adam. But he didn't. "Surely, how you live your life, how you treat your fellow human beings will determine your fate?"

"Of course, as long as you let the Lord guide you. Do not act unilaterally."

"Right, right. I'm with you now. Yeh, that's a bit clearer. Thanks."

"Delve into the gospels, why don't you? Satisfy yourself, friend, that their message is true," said the preacher.

"Sure thing, I'll catch up with you soon. By the way, where's your loudspeaker today?"

"Satan has robbed me of it, but he will never silence the word of the Lord."

Adam was left in a reflective mood. He still couldn't make up his mind if it was all a load of mumbo jumbo or if he really had stumbled across a faith that would change his life forever.

A week or so later Adam was leafing through the Arizona Daily Star newspaper when he caught sight of a short article at the foot of page 11:

"BODY DISAPPEARS FROM MORGUE.

"The body of Arnold Westerby, a homeless 46-year old born-again Christian, has disappeared from Tucson Morgue. Westerby, a native Texan, had lived in Tucson since 1978 and worked for the city council in the 1980s. He passed away suddenly, three days earlier. This is the first incident of its kind at the morgue and the staff is mystified. They are speculating that someone with an interest in selling organs on the black market may have stolen the body, but there was no sign of forced entry."

Adam could not believe his eyes. He sat staring at the page for ages. The news of the preacher's death knocked him for six. True, he had only seen the man twice, but that had been enough for him to realize that he was different. There had been a serenity about him; he seemed unaffected by the grind of everyday life.

Adam had felt a sense of security in his company. He knew that he was fortunate never to have suffered bereavement among his close family. But, now, for the first time, he experienced the pain of loss. He felt numb and empty. The whys and wherefores were as inscrutable as ever, but this kind soul had been summoned back to his maker's workshop, his earthly mission at an end. Adam had featured in the death throes of that mission, and he pondered on whether the preacher man's endeavors to enlighten him would really bear fruit.

A few days later, Adam was having breakfast at the Good Egg on Oracle and River. He was wolfing down his poached eggs on rye toast when he overheard a conversation between two bespectacled, academic looking guys at the next table.

They were talking about a TV program that one of them had seen about religion and faith. There had been a heated debate between an atheist and a deacon. The former was singing the praises of the philosopher Nietzsche, who famously argued that "God is dead," by which he meant that religion denies human beings their true nature as rational, active, creative beings and that God must therefore be "killed" if we want to do away with dogma and superstition and rediscover our real selves. The deacon's response was that man can never stand alone and has always been dependent on powers external to himself. Man's natural response to the solitariness of the human condition is to exercise his self and examine his soul through faith and prayer. Adam listened intently and found what they were saying extremely thought-provoking. After breakfast, he went for a stroll around Reid Park, one of his favorite places in Tucson. Circumnavigating its sizeable lake, home to a large variety of waterfowl, and lying in the shade of its Aleppo pines and eucalyptus trees next to its rock waterfall never failed to relax him.

He found himself re-running the conversation he'd just heard and resolved to start reading up on religion himself. It was about time he did some reading, period, he thought. He hadn't read a book for at least four years. The last one was Mario Puzo's The Godfather, a copy of which he'd found lying on the ground outside Starbucks on Grant and Swan. It was easy for Adam to lose himself in the park. Being there brought back many happy memories of his childhood. He, his mom, dad, sister, and grandpa would have picnics there at least twice a year. They would roast their weenies and make wonderful hot dogs with fresh coleslaw, jalapenos, and guacamole, all smothered in A1 steak sauce. And they would always bring their portable outdoor basketball system with them and have competitions.

Grandpa was six foot three and had played for a successful Wildcats team that had won back to back Border Conference titles after the war. He'd had a reputation for possessing one of the meanest no-look passes in the game. Adam would never forget the time Grandpa tried one at Reid Park. The ball had hit a passing Mexican woman on her ample butt and caused her to drop a whole tray of tamales. She had a fit and only calmed down when Dad gave her ten bucks. Even then, she walked off cursing and gesticulating wildly.

Adam walked around the zoo. He'd been going to zoos his whole life and had always been transfixed by the creatures there. Reid Park Zoo had some amazing species. Not least, the huge five hundred pound Aldabra tortoise, the capybara, a giant guinea pig lookalike, which the accompanying information plaque said is the world's biggest rodent, and his all-time favorite, the giant anteater with its long, tapered snout, housing a pencil-thin, eel-like tongue that extended to two feet. Adam had once won a fancy dress competition dressed as one. It was on the same night he'd kissed a girl for the first time. Ever since then, the anteater had been his lucky charm, and he'd used anteater key chains, boxers, socks, and, the piece de resistance, his genuine anteater skull.

It had taken Adam a year to face up to reality. He was up to his neck in debt, fifty-five grand to be specific. His house had been foreclosed on, his car had been repossessed, and his long-term girlfriend had walked as soon as the writing was on the wall. He'd moved back in with his parents and had no social life to speak of. But the positive thing was that he'd finally taken the plunge and filed Chapter 7 bankruptcy. It had not been at all painful. In fact, it had felt positively therapeutic, like spilling out a long held dirty secret. The endless calls and dunning notices would soon end. Finally, there was light at the end of the tunnel. The prospect of a debt free life felt good, very good.

Adam's father had talked him into going to L.A. to meet a friend of his who ran an expanding bathroom company. They were looking for dynamic sales and marketing people, their advertisement said, with the potential to earn between fifty and seventy grand a year apparently. Adam was not in the slightest bit interested but had agreed to an interview just to get his dad off his back. Adam was finding it very tough to motivate himself when it came to work. He just couldn't see himself going back to nine to five employment. He had begun to consider that perhaps there was another way to live. He was the first to admit that he enjoyed money, and he had never been one of those who argued that money could not buy you happiness. But real money had eluded him so many times, always remaining tantalisingly out of reach. This last debacle had made him think that perhaps it was just not meant to be. At the interview, Adam had done his best to appear interested, but he was sure the man could see through him. Even as Adam was assuring him that he knew how to close a deal, he felt like a fraud.

On the flight back to Tucson, Adam was immersed in his thoughts. Drifting in and out of sleep he didn't notice the priest slip into the empty seat beside him. He did the mother of all double takes when he set eyes on him. What was going on? He'd never met a man of the cloth in his life. Yet now religion seemed to be pursuing him relentlessly.

"Father, would you mind if I asked you a question?"

"Not at all, young man, go ahead."

"Well, it's just that I've been thinking a lot about your religion recently, and I met a Christian preacher who died a few weeks ago. I read that his body had disappeared from the morgue. Next, I overhear a conversation about religion which intrigued me, and now you come and sit next to me. Something is drawing me towards believing, but I'm confused. I've always considered myself to be a practical, logical, rational sort of person. I never believe anything unless I see it with my own eyes. I have never been convinced that there is a God or another world after this one. What makes you believe in God? How can you be so sure there is anything up there?" concluded Adam, as he raised his eyes to the heavens and gestured upward with his index finger.

"Well, for more than twenty centuries, millions of our fellow human beings, including some of the greatest minds ever to walk the earth, have followed the path of the righteous, of our Lord Jesus Christ. Could it be possible that all of them have been so gullible as to have been taken in by the story of a humble carpenter from Galilee? The path is long and arduous, but we are resolute and shall find salvation. The hardest journey of all is a mere three inches. It is the one from your head to your heart. Do not understand so that you can believe. Believe first and then understand."

"I see what you mean, father." Adam screwed his face up as he sought to make sense of the priest's words. Was it just that he liked the sound of the words, the way the holy man spoke? Or was the message itself persuasive? No answers came in response, and the conversation with the man of God died abruptly, the priest nodding off to sleep, leaving Adam lost in his thoughts. He felt warm and surprisingly calm. For the first time in ages that gnawing sensation in the pit of his stomach was not there. It was as though he was embarking on a spiritual odyssey and such a prospect was a good deal more appetizing than a job selling bathrooms in L.A.

It was 9 a.m. on a Wednesday. Adam was giving a speech on the virtues of wealth creation and trickle-down theory to five hundred businessmen and women. The phone ringing denied his dream the chance to reach its conclusion.

"Mr. Pritchard?"

"Don't tell me, Capital One Bank."

"No, we're HSBC actually. It's about your computer payments. You're five months in arrears."

"Yes, I know. I was just about to write to you actually. I filed Chapter 7 bankruptcy two days ago. My reference is B6813. Would you like more details?"

"Er, umm. Does this mean you will not be making any further payments?"

'You betcha. You are on my list of creditors so you'll be hearing from the trustees. Would you like the information?"

"No, it's okay. We'll wait to be formally notified."

"Very good. Thanks for calling."

"No problem. Bye."

The sense of closure was immensely satisfying. Once Adam had got over the pride thing there wasn't all that much to it. He had lost his apartment, car, and all the trappings of middle class respectability, but he truly felt like he had cast off his chains. Suddenly, life was so much simpler. He no longer had to worry about business plans, inventories, re-mortgaging, and all the rest of it. Adam's concerns nowadays were a good deal more rudimentary. He relished the things in life which were wholesome and nourishing. For the first time since his childhood he had begun to notice the minutiae of the world around him: the smell of freshly cut grass, the squirrel scurrying up the bark of a tree, the dawn chorus, and the wonderfully authentic feel of a fountain pen nib on high quality, vellum paper.

Does God exist? Adam was uncertain, but he'd dipped his toe in the water and, from a starting point deep in the wilderness, this was tantamount to a giant leap forward.

www.ingramcontent.com/pod-product-compliance
Lightning Source LLC
Chambersburg PA
CBHW020404030726
47496CB00007B/2297